MW01518464

got★no★secrets

GOT NO SECRETS

stories by danila botha

Tightrope Books

Copyright © Danila Botha, 2010.

ALL RIGHTS RESERVED. No part of this publication may be repro-
duced, stored in a retrieval system, or transmitted, in any form
or by any means, without prior permission of the publisher or, in
the case of photocopying or other reprographic copying, a licence
from Access Copyright, the Canadian Copyright Licensing Agency.
www.accesscopyright.ca, info@accesscopyright.ca

Tightrope Books
602 Markham Street
Toronto, Ontario
Canada M6G 2L8
www.tightropebooks.com

Canada Council
for the Arts

Conseil des Arts
du Canada

ONTARIO ARTS COUNCIL
CONSEIL DES ARTS DE L'ONTARIO

EDITOR: Shirarose Wilensky
COPYEDITOR: Chris Edwards
COVER DESIGN: Karen Correia Da Silva
TYPESETTING: Shirarose Wilensky

Produced with the assistance of the Canada Council for the Arts and
the Ontario Arts Council.

Printed in Canada.

LIBRARY AND ARCHIVES CANADA CATALOGUING IN PUBLICATION

Botha, Danila
    Got no secrets / Danila Botha.

Short stories.
ISBN 978-1-926639-08-6

    I. Title.

PS8603.O915G58 2010   C813.6   C2009-907128-2

For my grandfather Jonah,
who believed in me before I did.

And for my husband Steve,
who gives me, and is, everything.

I have no secrets anymore.

CONTENTS

PARADOX

I'm hungry, I'm dirty
I'm losing my mind, everything's fine!
I'm freezing, I'm starving
I'm bleeding to death, everything's fine!
—"Mother, Mother," Tracy Bonham

IT'S UNBELIEVABLY HOT ALL OF A SUDDEN. THE SUN IS BEATING down on me, hitting me directly in the eyes. When I look up all I see is the dull grey of everything—the buildings, the sidewalk, the garbage cans behind me. If this is what it's like to come down, all I want to do is go back up. I wait for my head to stop pounding. I rest it between my legs and, for a second, it feels good—until I remember I'm wearing a skirt. It's broad daylight now, 8:30 in the morning and my lace underwear is in full view of a busy intersection.

I can't remember last night.

Tina comes running out of the alleyway and when she does I feel the effects of everything that happened—the colours around her blur and she seems to be coming at me. If I didn't know her, I swear, for a second I'd be scared shitless.

We get going. She's hungover and seconds a way from throwing up—huge chunks of I-don't-know-what on my favourite pair of Converse. It's a smell I'll never get rid of, no matter how many times I wash them. I ask her between gulps if she remembers any details. It scares me that hours of last night are gone from my mind. I mean, if I blacked out I'd remember, right? She shakes her head. She remembers the first dealer, his house, and the creepy rail thin guy waiting out front. She remembers the first rave, the stupid fifteen-year-olds with their ridiculous bright clothes and huge pacifiers. I only remember a girl we met, Jamie, and some of her friends she introduced us to. They were really nice—gave us E—two pills each, and we didn't even have to do anything.

I remember the two guys we went off with, dancing and screaming down the street at three in the morning. I remember thinking that rum and Coke and the lollipops they'd given out at the club were the best tasting things on earth. I don't know what happened next, but I know we must have just come from a dealer's 'cause there's one just down the street. I don't know what we had just tried, but it had to have been good 'cause I don't even have money left for cab fare.

I tell Tina that next time we should bring a camera. After a long pause she slurs that the kind of things we do you gotta charge for. That's why I love her. She's funny, even when she's loaded.

I TAKE THE SUBWAY DOWN TO MY PARENTS' HOUSE IN MIDTOWN. I understand why the train has earned the name the Vomit Comet. I miss my stop twice. By the time I get home, it's a quarter to ten and no one's there. I make myself a glass of hot water with lemon and take the vitamins my mother has left out for me on the counter. I take a bath and nearly fall asleep. I consider throwing out my shoes, then I realize that one of my parents might see them in the garbage. I find a pair of grey pants, slacks really, very grown-up, and a white shirt that's loose enough to be almost demure. I feel like Alicia Silverstone in the movie *Clueless*. I'm wearing my most responsible-looking outfit.

I find the note my mother left me as I head out the door, then I remember: I have a test this afternoon. I grab the textbook that's been sitting on my bathroom counter for two months as I race out the door. I'm suddenly worried that I'm going to be late.

On the subway I glance over the pages. I think I heard somewhere that if you cram it's all short-term memory. I'm definitely screwed then because I think I've heard that drugs deplete short-term memory.

I get there just in time to see people panicking outside the classroom, anxiously trying to cram for the two-essay, five-short-answer test worth thirty percent of our final mark. I find my friend Sam who congratulates me on how calm I look.

"You look confident," she tells me, squeezing my arm just below my elbow.

"I am," I tell her, smiling tightly. I'm confident that I don't know the material and that it's way, way too late to start freaking out. I write the test in an hour and a half and hand it in. I don't know how I did, but I hope I passed. If I did it'll be a small miracle.

I decide to actually go to my next class, so I walk all the way across campus to the psychology building. We're discussing Jung and his theories on the collective unconscious. Well, that's a lie. Almost a thousand of us are being talked down to about Jung. I watch as perfectly interesting ideas become dry and pointless in a matter of seconds. I reach into my bag for my notebook and, out of guilt, begin taking notes.

IT'S 7:30 AND THE CLASS IS OVER. I WALK ACROSS CAMPUS TO a nearby restaurant where my friend Cosby works. He's the most rational person I know. He's not privileged like me. His parents can't afford to pay his tuition, so he works two jobs. He reminds me of it every day.

He reaches behind the counter and slops some rice onto a plate, then hands it to me. I'm a vegan, and rice is about the only thing I can eat at Joe's BBQ Grill. I thank him and sit down at a nearby counter. I realize it's the first thing I've had to eat in about two days.

My mother calls me immediately after dinner. My cellphone's ring beats at my brain like a jackhammer. Even though I have call display, I pick it up, just to make it shut up. My mom doesn't know about anything that goes on in my life. She doesn't know what subjects I'm taking, what I like studying, what I do any night of the week. She never asks any questions. She just wants to know that her investment is working out well—that her daughter will one day become a respected professional who is actually worth something. I hope I don't live that long.

I tell her that I'm fine, that the test went well, that I'm going to have to spend another night at the library. Another project for my abnormal psychology class. A lot of research. Periodicals, you know. I'll probably see her in the morning, maybe.

I can't believe she buys it. I can't believe she never wonders where I am. I wish, just once, she would worry about me. I hang up, and feel like one of those men who always lie to their wives about what they really do late at night at the office. But then I force the thought out of my head. You can choose your partner, you can choose your friends. You sure as hell can't choose your family.

I storm off into the bathroom, wash my hands, and call Tina. I suddenly need to not think so much.

She's here within fifteen minutes, a speed demon even when she's sober. I get in the car and we drive off. I don't know where we're going, but I know it's only a matter of time before I feel better. I want to feel so much better that I can forget what it's like to have so many feelings I can't do anything with.

Tina asks what's wrong, and I tell her it's my mom. "Ah, Clarisse," Tina says, imitating my mom's French accent. My mom is about as French as Madonna is British. Well, okay, that's not true, she was actually born in France. She just happens to have lived in Canada for about thirty-five years now.

Back in France my mom's family was established and successful. Here, thanks to my dad, they're the *nouveau riche*. My parents have always put pressure on me to surpass them financially. They care more about my grades than my happiness, so they've always paid a fortune to send me to the best schools. Having a mom who's French doesn't make you any more able to speak the language. I should know. She sent me to French Immersion for ten years and I can still hardly speak a damn word of it.

Tina persists with wanting to know what's wrong, wanting to hear about my problems, and I'm starting to get annoyed.

"It is what it is, Tin," I say through closed teeth. There's no point in talking about it.

I stare out the window. We pass restaurants and bars and people congregated in groups on the sidewalk. I wonder what they're on. We keep driving and I watch as the trees turn into poles covered in flyers about parties and the buildings turn into abandoned warehouses perfect for raves. I have no idea where we are. I don't even ask anymore, I just let Tina take me wherever she wants to go.

WE PICK UP TWO GUYS ON THE SIDEWALK WHO HOLLER AT US. They're on their way downtown, to King and Spadina, near where our dealer lives. They're yelling generic shit at us, like "Hey baby, wanna get down?" and "Nice legs," when Tina stops the car and invites them to get in. Up close they're not even cute, but she says she has a feeling about them. She's always right. They've got the goods, even though I wish I didn't have to touch them. They're kind of greasy-looking: too much hairspray, shirts that are a little too tight. I don't say anything; my body feels really tense.

One guy introduces himself as Tony and starts giving me a massage. The other guy says he's Johnny and slips something under my tongue. I wonder if Tina can see what I'm seeing: the seats start glowing and Mike or Bob or Tony or whoever has about eight arms like an octopus. Suddenly I want him so badly, and I jump on him and stare into his eyes, which are shooting rainbows, and at his mouth, which is shooting blood. The floor moves under my feet. This is so cool.

Tina pulls over into a parking lot, swerving and barely missing the sidewalk. We park, I don't know for how long, and I spend some quality time with the other guy. It's really bad, the acid is wearing off, and all I want to do is cry. He reminds me of a doll my sister had as a kid: beady eyes, plastic cheeks. I kick the back door open and practically fall out of the car. I feel it coming up and soon I'm barfing, getting some on the seat, on my skirt, on my tights, and a whole lot on the sidewalk. My hair falls into my mouth, my hands are dirty, and I smell so bad. I want to fall down onto the concrete and lie there in my own mess. I want to die out here, my face scraped by the gravel, my body touched by strangers, my best friend oblivious.

Tina gets out of the car, walks around, and helps me up. We head into what the guys call an underground club. Really it's just a hole in the ground with bad techno music that makes the floorboards bang. It's dank and dark and there are some people talking, but I have no idea what they're saying.

MY HEAD HURTS THE NEXT MORNING AND NO AMOUNT OF ADVIL or grapefruit or herbal tea can fix it. I keep partying like a maniac for days, weeks maybe. I go to random clubs, hook up with guys whose faces I don't recognize five minutes later, and do more drugs than I can keep track of. I think I go through thousands of dollars. Somehow I still get up, talk to people, and sometimes go to class. My body goes into total autopilot. It's amazing how little my brain needs me to function. I walk by the psychology lab, the one that I haven't been near in weeks. I see the grades posted on the door. It takes me a while to find my name: Barnes, Jennifer. It hits me right away—that test I thought I'd passed? I'd failed. It disturbs me how little I care.

I WAKE UP ONE DAY TO A PHONE CALL FROM MY FATHER. I DON'T even know what day of the week it is. I think it's Sunday 'cause *The Simpsons* is on at eight. It's the one where they go to Brazil. Homer keeps asking for Brazil nuts, and they tell him that here, we just call them nuts. Being stoned makes everything so much funnier.

Even though my dad and my mom are still together, he never calls me. People ask me all the time if I even have a father. I wish I had a father who called me all the time, wanting to hear about my problems and what makes me happy. My dad just wants to talk about money. He wants to know how it's possible for me to have gone through so much, so fast. I just want to know how I can get more off him. He gets angry really quietly, so that if you didn't know him you'd have no idea what was coming. He doesn't get emotional and yell and scream like my mother. He loses his temper in carefully calculated doses.

In a flat tone he tells me exactly how much money I've gone through in the past three weeks. I fumble and make excuses. I give him a line about new textbooks, bullshit him about library fines. I tell him I needed new shoes for running track. He doesn't buy it. He tells me that I'm lazy and irresponsible.

"You're nowhere near as smart as you think you are, Jennifer," he says. "You need to find another man to provide for you—but that shouldn't be too hard since you've always had a hard time keeping your legs shut."

I can never think of an answer fast enough. I open my mouth like I'm about to say something, then close it. He softens his tone. He tells me to go out and get a job, that even though I'll have my own practice as a psychologist one day I need to help support myself now.

What about what I want? I want to tell him that the last place I want to be right now, or ever, is in school. I want to point out the number of psychology graduates who'll probably end up driving taxis. Besides, the last thing I should ever do is help other people with their problems. But instead I tell him that between all my classes I have no extra time to work.

"Aren't my grades and my future important to you?" I ask. He doesn't even answer. Shit, no wonder all the guys I've ever dated have been feminine. Stoic and in control, my ass.

I tell him I'll look for a job, and I find one by the end of the week. I'm a waitress at Crocodile Jay's, a pool hall just off campus. It's disturbingly tame. Guys knock back two beers on a Tuesday night and think they're being really bad. Worse than the boredom is the money: $6.25 an hour plus tips is hardly enough to cover my expenses. One dose of E is at least ten bucks a pop. I quit after a week.

Tina wants to celebrate my quitting with a trip to a new friend's downtown. It's a tiny apartment with no heating, and we stand in the dingy hallway shivering in our short skirts. By the time the dealer gets there—'cause, let's face it, we have no friends—I'm so desperate to get inside that I agree to try it. I know that blow is bad. I know that once you start it you never come off, but, fuck, how bad can it be? I've always wanted to be thinner—look at all those models from the nineties. I've always wanted to take risks, have fun.

My entire week's salary is gone on just one flap. It's like magic. Fairy dust that goes straight from my nose to my brain. I feel it tingling like my blood vessels are popping. I feel it in my arms and legs, and then I feel it in my veins. It makes the whole room—the carpet, the lamp, the closet— feel like it's coming toward me, but not in a way that's scary. It makes me feel like the whole room is hugging me, wanting to come close, wanting to touch me. It's the most intense thing I've ever tried, it makes me want to open up and talk and talk. It makes me feel warmer, more confident. In a strange way, it makes me feel more alive. For some reason it makes me think of the grade-ten definition I'd learned for the word *paradox*: every day of our lives we are one step closer to death.

Suddenly I'm laughing hysterically. I am literally the definition of the term.

Seeing how much I loved it, the dealer asks me when I'm coming back for more. I'm pretty out of it, but I think I tell him I can't afford it. At least I hope that's what I said. He asks me where I live, and when I tell him at my parents' house he laughs like it's the funniest thing he's ever heard.

"Don't you want to be independent, get your own place, maybe drop out of school?" he asks.

It all sounds so good I don't know what to say. The dealer is the one person looking out for me. The dealer has my happiness all figured out. I have some hazy thought about his job being all about science if he makes the drugs, so it makes sense that he's figured out my formula. Drugs make me feel less alone. Drugs help me realize what I want.

I get up shakily and tell him I want some more. Tina is about to pass out, sprawled on his soft brown couch. Her body twitches lightly. He leads me into the next room, where there is no light except for the computer screen. You could make a lot of money on the Internet, he tells me.

I GO BACK THE NEXT DAY, AND THE DAY AFTER THAT. POSING for the webcam is quick and, in a way, painless. Everything is painless now.

I bring a guy home and we smoke crack in my bedroom, rolling around, making out, and knocking things over. I'm having a pretty good time until we're interrupted by my mother's yelling and look of total horror. I'm not that high, so I tell her to calm the fuck down. My father picks me up by my jean jacket and throws me out of the house. I smell the Absolut Citron on his breath as he slams me into the garage door. My head bangs against the wood, but I hardly feel it. I stand shivering in the driveway for ten minutes before I realize I have to find a pay phone to call a cab. I have no idea where Tina is, and the guy stands beside me dazed and useless. He reaches over to give me a hug, but his hand slips down onto my ass. He tries to grab it and I move away. I'm not in the mood.

"Babe," he says, slurring, not looking at me.

This sucks. I don't want to talk to him ever again. I never want to be back here.

I GET THAT APARTMENT AND SHARE IT WITH TINA. I DON'T officially drop out, I just stop going to class. I do it until I flunk out, and no one's around to make me feel guilty. Tina's strung out so often it's like living alone. I look at her: bone thin where she once had boobs and hips, black mascara running down her face, her once perfect hair peroxide blond with roots. I wonder if she knows she's a junkie. She has all these sexy clothes, but she doesn't even get dressed anymore. She just uses and poses for our webcam. She inserts anything. I once saw her stick a stiletto heel up there, for a guy with a foot fetish. She invites anyone over and does whatever she's told. She shoots up now.

"Relax," Andrew, our dealer and friend, tells me. His tone is soft and seductive. "There's a whole niche for girls like her."

Soon she's featured shooting up on cokewhores.com. One night she goes out and doesn't come back until two days later. Andrew tells me she was walking the street. She doesn't talk to me anymore, doesn't tell me anything. I guess I have nothing to offer her.

I always thought there was a lot of money to be made that way, a lot per hour. Andrew tells me I should join an agency, where I could make up to $150 a pop. I like money, but I don't want to move. Getting up off the couch hurts. My body is bruised and when I look in the mirror for the first time in weeks I don't recognize the person staring back. My eyes are bloodshot, sunken in, and black underneath. My skin is sallow and my hair is plastered to the sides of my face. My body is so thin. I thought that would have made me happy, but I don't feel anything.

I've forgotten what it's like to feel anything at all. I stare out the window. All everyone wants, I think, is to feel, to experience, to really see. But when you actually do, you realize something: it's really not that exciting. You can fill your life with more and more, but you can be left with less than what you started with.

I get up and look at Andrew. First I smile, and then I'm laughing. It beats the hell out of crying.

JESUS WAS A PUNK ROCKER

I REALLY HAVE TO TAKE A PISS.

I have to piss, but I can't, because I'm lying on my back, legs spread, and I can't get up.

My bed is collapsing. The planks of wood holding up my mattress have snapped in half one by one. It happened slowly over a few months. I felt the last one break this morning, just before I woke up. That's what happens when you buy a bed from Ikea. Think like a student, get the back of a geriatric woman.

I reach onto my side table for a cigarette. It hurts to sit up, so I don't. I look down to find that I'm still wearing my jeans from the night before. I'm glad. It means I have matches in my pocket. I smoke a cigarette staring at the ceiling.

I still have to piss, so I grab the vase next to my bed that once held eighteen long-stemmed red roses. It's been empty for a while. I undo my fly and peel my jeans off. I manage to take care of business without getting a single drop on my sheets—a small miracle, since it's a long thin vase, made of glass. I briefly consider sending it to him, with a note: *This is what a sincere sentiment looks like, asshole.*

I finally get up. It's 8:35 a.m. I'm going to be late.

I step into the shower, turn the water on to the hottest it can get. I use my foot pumice to scrape the stamps off the backs of my hands, the ones that tell me what clubs or bars I went to last night. Apparently I went to the Horseshoe, and the Rivoli. My hair is greasy and stinks of smoke. I douse it in shampoo, wash it twice, then rinse like crazy.

I don't eat because I can't. I still have vomit lodged in the back of my throat, between my teeth, under my tongue. No amount of rinsing will get the taste out. I feel like I need to run through a car wash, clean the crevices, the part of me that can't seem to get clean. I can't remember anything, which worries me. I need an eternal cleansing of my spotless mind. I need to remember, and then erase.

I have fifteen minutes to get to a place that's forty-five minutes away. I find my clothes, then my shoes, and race down the street to grab a taxi. My scrubs, as always, are wrinkled, and I've lost my name tag.

I get the joke about nurses in porn a lot, so I fucking hate it that the smart-ass taxi driver tells me I'm the kind of good-looking nurse that could be a star. I have no idea what cheesy movies with bleached blondes with fake tits and equally fake moans have to do with work that's exhausting and not glamorous at all. My job means I'm constantly reassuring people, which makes me feel better about my own life, but only temporarily. A lot of people complain about

the hectic pace of Toronto hospitals, but I like it. I like working ten- to eleven-hour days. The busier my hands are, the
less likely I am to do something stupid, to over-think, or
make a bad decision. I've spent ninety-nine percent of my
life over-thinking everything. I once had a fight with a friend
who said I mull over things until they don't exist anymore.
He was right, that used to be true. I used to consider and
discuss everything until I drove everyone away. My mission
in life is to not think so much, and I take it very seriously.

I put my headphones on so the taxi driver will stop talking to me. It works for most of the trip. I blast punk, like the
Ramones and Black Flag, bands that were my favourites in
high school and, for a minute, it makes me smile. I used to
draw their logos in black ink on the insides of my arms until
I was old enough to get tattoos.

I stare out the window and notice some teenagers skate-
boarding. It makes me feel like I'm seven years old again,
with my nose pressed to the window of a toy store the day
before Christmas, knowing I won't get any presents because
my parents are Jews. I mean, how terrible is that? I always
hated being Jewish. Chosen People, my ass. Cheap People
is more like it. Other kids got dolls and books and bikes,
and all I got was mouldy chocolate, wrapped up in gold foil
to look like money. My parents never believed in Hanuk-
kah presents either. They're Orthodox. They believed that
presents took away from the spirit of the holiday, turned
something Jewish and wonderful into something Christian

and terrible. It never made sense to me, even then.

When I see these carefree kids skating now, it gets to me in the same way, the injustice of it. Three years ago I could get drunk in parks, make out with strangers in the middle of the day, buy cheap wine that tasted like sunshine in a bottle. Now I have to be responsible. Now I have to think ahead. I hate the financial responsibility that comes with being able to move out of my parents' house and party as much as I want. I could eat ice cream for breakfast, but I can't quit the job I hate so much because I'd be out on the street. My parents would rather eat used condoms they found on the sidewalk than help me. I'm the biggest disgrace my family has ever seen. They pray for the day I get married and change my last name, or just get it legally changed, so nobody knows I'm theirs. Sometimes I can understand how they feel. I'm unconventional and strange, and they're deeply conservative. I've embraced my freakishness, while they cower and hide from it.

When I was in high school I was angry all the time. I talked back to teachers, skipped class, and got kicked out when I did go. I was a rebel. When I graduated and went to college, I decided I wanted to try to challenge the system from the inside. I realized that was pointless after I got fired three times. Now I'm just a regular clock-punching employee with sensible black shoes. Most days, when I look at myself I feel like a hypocrite and a jackass. My job is supposed to be fulfilling, but it's exhausting. I'm not in any position to help people, but I have to act like I am, act like a professional. If they only knew me, if they knew what my life was really like, they'd never trust me to do anything.

People open up to me because I don't look like a typical nurse. I have six earrings and eight tattoos you can sometimes see, depending on what I'm wearing. My nail polish is always black and chipping. I have nose and labret piercings, but I take them out for work. My boss hates the way I look, I can tell, but patients relate to me better than they do to other nurses. I tell them to call me Mack, instead of Mackenzie, or Ms Moore. I go out of my way to make them feel at home, so that they open up to me, so that they tell me the truth. I can't help them if I don't know what's really going on. I hear a lot of crazy stories, but I never tell them anything about myself, even when they ask. They wouldn't want to know, anyway.

WHEN I FINALLY GET TO THE HOSPITAL I JUMP OUT OF THE CAB and speed up the stairs as fast as I can. Despite the fact that I'm thin, which is another of my serious obsessions, I'm winded by the time I get to the fourth floor. I am totally unfit. The head nurse, my boss, Mary, yells at me for being late. I have patients to see in fifteen minutes and I have no time to review their files. She grabs me by the arm so hard I wince.

I only have five minutes to go to the bathroom. I duck into the stall and roll up my sleeves. I always wear a long-sleeved shirt under my scrubs. I take the Swiss Army knife out of the back of my left shoe, where it's covered by my pants.

I don't remember how old I was the first time I cut myself. I was in my parents' kitchen, and I was having a really bad day. I wanted to eat ice cream, but we didn't have any. Plus, it would have made me really sick anyway—I'm allergic to dairy. I decided to be good and started slicing one of those awful, healthy vegetables—I think it was a red pepper. I took a bite and it tasted like shit, so I figured it had to be good for me. I was concentrating on the taste, wondering if I should've just taken a multi-vitamin instead, when I accidentally sliced my fucking palm open. It was so gross. I spread my fingers open in front of me. I bled all over and didn't even feel it. The blood spilled onto the white counter and I stared at it for at least a minute. Finally, I ran into the bathroom, grabbed a towel and held it there. I applied pressure to the wound, cleaned it with iodine, and put a couple of Band-Aids over it.

I felt so good—I'd made a mess that I'd managed to clean up. I had taken care of myself and the situation. I didn't even feel the pain—so I just kept doing it. I have scars up and down my arms now—puffy red lines that poke out of the flesh, scabs that have no desire to heal. I'm young—I bet they'd heal eventually if I just gave them a chance. Maybe one day.

My legs look fucked up, too, because I went through a burning phase. I threw hot oil from a frying pan onto my thighs for a couple of months. It hurt like hell so I didn't do it for long. People used to say my legs were my best feature. I never saw it. But now there's something beautiful about them—like I decided how they'd look, like I'm in control.

I cut myself every day, sometimes twice or even three times a day if I have a lot of stress. It gives me a release like nothing else. It helps me feel real, brings my anxieties and fears down to earth—it makes me feel like I'm taking all the shit I feel on the inside and putting it in a place I can see it, so I never forget it. If someone hurts me, I never forget it now. If a guy betrays me, even if I try to forget, my body will always have the scar.

I've been even more of a wreck ever since the guy I fell in love with decided he didn't want to be with me anymore. He had these liquid brown eyes that just seemed to melt even more every time he talked to me about something serious. He was so intense and so passionate. He was kind—gave change to the homeless, made small talk with everyone, even strangers. He made me want to be a lot nicer, a lot more conscious of how I treated people. He challenged me intellectually. He was everything I ever wanted, and even though I hadn't had a steady boyfriend since I was in grade eleven, I just wanted to be his. I wanted to belong to him more than anything in the world.

He thought I was nice, too, just not anything special. I didn't make his knees weak like he did mine. I didn't make him want to pen bad poetry, or think about nothing else for hours while he lay in the bath, getting wrinkled fingers. I was just a passing fancy for him.

His last words to me were, "I think you're a nice girl, but . . ."

I never even heard the rest of the sentence.

I had never tried so hard to be what I thought someone else wanted me to be. For the first time in my life, I really wanted to be good, I wanted to be loved. It's physical: I want him to love me so much, I can feel it in every part of my body. But there's nothing I can do about it.

I've tried sleeping with other guys to get over it, but it doesn't help. It sometimes feels empowering, like I'm starting to get over it, but it usually just makes me hate myself more. I have no idea how many guys I've slept with in total now, I lost track after ninety-nine. By which I mean the year, not the number. What scares me is if I counted, I'd find I've slept with way more than a hundred guys. So I ignore it. I lie to men. I told him the truth, and look where it got me. Most of the time, being myself hurts me more than anything. It's easier to be what I think, or even know, people want.

ONCE I GET OUT OF THE BATHROOM, THE DAY PASSES BY IN A blur. I'm in the ER and then the psych ward. I see addicts and teenagers. I skip lunch and see more mental cases. I scribble notes in pencil and promise myself I'll rewrite them tomorrow. I even make a list of their files so I can do it the next day.

I see a guy who tried to kill himself by swallowing lots of Tylenol 3. His mother looks genuinely distressed and worried. I wish my parents cared that much.

I stop at Wendy's on my way home. I just want to stuff my face. There's something about grease, about knowing that I'm doing something bad for me, that feels so good sometimes. I mean, I know how bad it is. I paid to see that documentary about that guy who eats nothing but McDonald's for a month then nearly dies. But, on the other hand, it tastes amazing. I can eat and be full for less than five bucks. I had a friend who worked at Taco Bell who said all fast food restaurants use Grade F meat. It makes me wonder if I'm eating a Chihuahua right now. Oh well. At least if I die tomorrow, I successfully avoided lung cancer and liver failure, partied a lot, and don't have to go back to work or pay rent. At least, for once, I actually managed to save money.

I have plans tonight with a guy I met who's a little younger, but really into me. Even though I don't like him like that, it's an ego boost. It feels really good sometimes to be wanted. Plus, if I remember right, the sex was decent. At least I hope so.

I go home and put on some tough-looking jewellery and my studded belt. I line my eyes with black and wear a see-through studded mesh top with a black bra underneath. I feel slut-tastic.

We meet at the Reverb at Queen and Bathurst at eleven. An all-ages punk show was his idea, and I thought it might make me feel better. Reconnect me with my past.

The walls are plastered with homemade flyers for bands I've never heard of. I feel so old and out of touch. We catch the second-last band and the headliner. They're ska punk. The music's loud and thrashing. It just sounds like noise to me. I never thought that this would happen to me so soon. I gulp down a Scotch on the rocks and stare at the kids around me. They're wearing Ramones T-shirts they probably bought at Bluenotes. It's funny—I see Dead Kennedys T-shirts, skulls, and studded belts, but I feel no connection to these kids.

A fourteen-year-old stops me at the bar and asks me if I can buy her and her friends some drinks. I'm drunk myself so I say sure, why not? I get them some beer—a pitcher for four little girls—and keep walking. They stop me and ask if I want to share some, and even though it's crappy draft, I say yes.

I wonder if I was like them at their age. I wonder if I seem like a mom or a dinosaur to them. We sit in their booth and talk. They ask me how old I am, and when I tell them, the blonde says I give them hope. When they're twenty-seven, she says, they want to be like me. I don't want to tell them how I'm faking my way through every second of my life, including this conversation. I keep ordering more drinks until none of us knows what we're saying.

"To be punk all you have to do is be a rebel," one of them says. "Everyone you've ever liked is punk," she continues. "I mean, if you think about it, even Jesus was a punk rocker."

She is giddy with excitement. I shake my head.

"He was such a blue-collar, working-class hero. He was a badass: drinking a lot, like us, hanging with whores. He took the ultimate hit for standing by his ideals. Everyone must have thought he was insane."

I tell them it's time to go. They try to high five me, but I move away so fast I nearly elbow a girl in the face. This religion stuff is starting to freak me out. I need to get the fuck out of here.

My date and I stumble down the street. He puts his arm and around me as I puke all over the sidewalk—booze and water and my burger come up in chunks. I look up and see neon signs and store windows spinning. I see Young Thailand with its purple and yellow lettering and rotting yellow steps. I see the crack house beside it.

He walks me to my door, and I puke on his shoes, so he doesn't ask to come upstairs and I don't offer. I fall up the first five flights of stairs, then take the elevator up another seven flights. At least for once I'm here alone. My head is pounding like a jackhammer. I lie down and squeeze my temples. I'm going to be hungover tomorrow—again.

WHEN I WAKE UP IT'S LATE AND I CAN'T EVEN WALK STRAIGHT. I take another cab to work. At this rate I'll be broke by the end of the week—six days before I get my next paycheque. I hate my life.

I see a bunch of patients I forget immediately, until I

meet a kid called Jared. He's nine, and three months ago he lost his sister in a freak accident. His mom took them to an amusement park and they all went on a rollercoaster. Kelly had been sitting in the back, behind them both. Suddenly they heard a crash. His mother started yelling, begging someone to stop the ride. He assumed she'd dropped her purse. When he and his mom got out, he realized Kelly had fallen. He saw the height she'd fallen from. He had to see his sister in a bloody, tangled mess, her glasses smashed, her face smeared and bleeding. He had to live with the fact that if she'd been sitting where he was, she would have been fine. This beautiful nine-year-old boy was blaming himself for his sister's death.

I can't stop myself from crying right there, in front of him. I feel so out of my depth. I recommend an art therapist who might be able to help him express his feelings. I feel so helpless, so useless, I just want to make myself hurt. I can't wait to get home and get into my kitchen. I duck into the staff bathroom with my knife. Just another few quick stabs around the ankle. I pull my pant leg farther down and pull my sock higher up. When I'm done I feel a little more relaxed, and I walk out smiling a little.

WHEN I GET HOME IT'S SO QUIET THAT IT HITS ME—I MISS HIM more than anything. I check my messages and—nothing. No email, no calls. A while ago I stopped bothering to keep in touch with friends. I don't even know who to call. I could call the dude from last night, but I'm embarrassed. I never keep their numbers anyway; what's the point?

I stare into the mirror behind my bed and decide I want to make a change. I start cutting my hair. I use the scissors on my knife that I use for opening the mail. After a while I'm not even looking. I hate having long hair. I've had it this long, past my shoulders, spilling onto my chest, for almost two years. It's stringy and falls into my eyes. I don't want to be pretty. It doesn't help. No matter how good they say I look, guys only want to sleep with me. No one ever wants to be with me; they can sense that I'm trouble and they stay away. I want my outside to reflect my inside. I want to be ugly, messy, undeserving of a second look, never mind love.

I light a cigarette, inhale, and stare at the ceiling. A lot of people say that when they cut themselves they feel more alive. Like their pain makes them feel more real. For me it's about being honest, showing people how hideous I really am.

I'm wildly cutting now, and my hair is building up in piles on the floor. I'm shocked at how disconnected I feel from my body. What's nice is that when I cut myself I don't think about anything. I don't feel sad at all. The scissors come dangerously close to my cheek. I look in the mirror. My cheek is bleeding, but I don't feel it. It takes the sight of the blood running down my face for me to know it's happening.

I tell myself that I'm a person of ideas. That I could start a revolution, change the world. I keep telling myself that it's not too late. But when I feel like being honest with myself, I point out that my disciples have lost interest and the only person who's ever understood me, the only equal I've ever known doesn't want me around. I wanted to be a renegade and here I am, as misunderstood as I was when I was fifteen. Only now, there's no excuse for the angst. Now, not only does no one understand, no one really cares.

I crawl under the blankets and close my eyes to keep from crying.

Half an hour later I hear my phone ring.

A TINY THUD

★

I'M LATE FOR EVERYTHING. MY EX-BOYFRIEND USED TO JOKE that I'd be late for my own funeral. He was almost right. I was fifteen minutes late for his. It's something I've never forgiven myself for—the kind of self-centeredness that he had accused me of but I just couldn't see until that moment. He would have been so angry—like I couldn't even show up to that on time. Like he wasn't important enough for me to bother. Except that he was. He was everything.

I WAKE UP IN THE MIDDLE OF THE NIGHT PANICKING. I HAVE nightmares about my teeth falling out, that I'm getting ready, the morning of the funeral, about to brush my teeth, when they start, one by one. First my molars, then all the way up to the eye teeth, and finally the front two. I run my wet fingers over them, and watch as they slip out, into the sink, then down the drain.

Or I'm in the shower, about to shampoo my hair when it starts falling out in clumps. By the time I get out I'm almost bald, with just a couple of small patches on the sides, looking like a cancer victim, staring at the water dripping off my new double chin (these days I eat nothing but mint chocolate chip ice cream).

My shrink says it's one of the most common dreams you can have, that it signifies loss of control. She says it's normal, smiles in a way that I'm sure she thinks is sympathetic, and pats my arm. There's something about having my panic attacks and fears reduced to a cliché or stereotype that really makes me want to knock *her* teeth out.

People don't understand what it's like to lose someone until they do. I'm twenty-two years young, so obviously, most people my age don't get it. I get a lot of blank stares, fake sympathy, and uncomfortable silences. People struggle with what to say, choke on words like they're cherry pits, spit them out, or try to swallow them. I want to tell them it's okay. That I'd be pretty naïve to believe there's anything anyone could say or do for me.

I spend a lot of time inside now, in my apartment. It's a bachelor on Queen, a tiny shoebox that overlooks Grange Park. It's where I moved after all hell broke loose.

HE LIVED DOWN THE STREET, IN A HOUSE ON TECUMSEH AT Bathurst. It was a brown brick house in a row of brown brick houses, with a motorcycle parked out front. It's that kind of neighbourhood. There's a sex shop around the corner where live models stand in the window in their underwear, waving to passersby, giving them a heart attack. They're all thin and

tall, with long blond or dark brown hair. They all have stom-
achs that are prettier than their faces, toned and tight, while
their eyes and mouths are characterless. Apparently, they
don't even get paid money. They get paid in lingerie. Which
sounds like a pretty shit deal to me.

When I moved in with him I tried to give the house some
character. I painted the walls in acrylic paint with designs
and song lyrics. I tried to make it feel like the home I always
wanted. Now the walls are white again.

We met when I was nineteen. I went to an art show with
a friend and was bored out of my mind. The thing that was
cool about him was that even though he was a big deal, he
totally acted like he wasn't, and you could tell that he wasn't
putting it on, that he meant it. He had perspective, not just
about his success, but about everything. No matter how
hard I tried, perspective was something I didn't have.

Whenever I felt really bad about life, he'd drive me to the
most dangerous parts of the city, pull over and stop on the
sketchiest streets. There'd be people picking through trash
cans, talking to themselves, foaming at the mouth, coming
down off some drug. There'd be girls begging for change,
wearing knee-high pleather boots and short-shorts. There'd
be people shooting up in alleyways right in front of us. We'd
walk by and the smell of piss would assault us.

One time we saw a girl about to do smack. She was
sitting on the lid of a Dumpster wearing shorts and a tank
top. She had run out of veins in her arms and her legs and

was about to shoot into her neck. It was like seeing a car accident in slow motion. I was fascinated, horrified, but riveted. We watched as she froze, waiting for it to kick in. She didn't move, didn't blink, didn't breathe. We thought she was going to die. Then the look of recognition crept back into her eyes. She got up, stumbled over to us and, arms shaking, asked us for money. He reached into his bag and pulled out an apple. Disgusted, she threw it back at us and skulked back into the alley.

When I was with him I was invincible. When I was with him, whatever was bothering me was trivial and silly. I loved him for being the first person to make me see that.

He stopped using about five years before he met me. By the time we were a couple, it took him ages to make a move, something I loved because it meant he respected me, but it also frustrated me beyond belief.

I loved his fingers—so long and bony. And I loved his inner arms, with the faded track marks. They gave him character, I told him. They made him look like an individual. But he was deeply ashamed of them. He wore long-sleeved shirts even in the summer, in the sweltering Toronto humidity. He'd turn the air on as high as he could. So I started wearing long sleeves too. No amount of kissing him better could take the deep purple scarring away. I wanted to love him enough to his past. I wanted to inject myself into his remaining working veins. I wanted him to love me enough to be normal, to deal with his problems head on and never look back.

I SLEEP DURING THE DAY NOW AND GO FOR WALKS AT NIGHT. I like the inherent dangers of the street at night—the homeless people screaming, the crusty punk kids trying to steal your wallet. The way I've been feeling lately, they make me feel less alone. They make me feel okay, like I'm less crazy then they are, and definitely more sober. Like there's still hope for me. Like there's still a long way to go before I hit rock bottom.

It's 3 a.m.—pitch black, but I can see the glowing red numbers on my alarm clock. I roll onto my right side and stick a foot over the edge of my bed. I have to go to the bathroom. I stumble, crash into the wall, and bring the bead curtain that hangs in the doorway down on top of me. I hit the floor and find that a couple of strands have wrapped themselves around my neck. Jesus, can you imagine what my tombstone would say? *Cause of death: Plastic beaded curtain with blue stars. It was the hippie way to go.* I brush them aside and stand up. I put on my shirt, with sweat stains in the armpits. I put on the same jeans that I've been wearing for two weeks straight. They're my nighttime jeans. I feel the dust along the sides of my shoes, and I try to brush it off, even though I can't really see it.

My apartment building is full of fluorescent lights, which are blinding at the best of times. I blink and squint when I get out the door. The OCAD building makes me wish I were blind. It's ugly—lots of red and yellow and white poles piled on top of each other, facing different directions. If you look at it from my window, it kind of looks like a thin, long-legged dog is having sex with the rest of the building. It's pretentious and fake-meaningful. It embodies everything I hate about art.

When I first moved to this street, I was so excited. I figured I'd meet artists like me—people who spend their time talking and searching for meaning. People who want to express themselves somehow, and maybe make the world better. People who aren't full of shit. People who are warm instead of cool. Outcasts like me.

But I was wrong. They're all full of shit. They're covered with tattoos and have piercings all over their faces. They look like they'd beat you up if you saw them in a dark alley. Or bore you to death with talk about obscure artists you never even wanted to hear about.

If I had any friends, though, they'd be bugging me, wanting to talk about stuff I don't want to discuss with anyone. I hate when people repeat stories second hand and get the details wrong. I hate the thought of someone I love being reduced to an anecdote in some loser friend of a friend's lame, drunken 1 a.m. story. My memories of him are sacred. They belong only to me.

Sometimes I dream about him. We're both alive, or we're both dead. I can see him like it just happened: the way he throws his head back and squints, then laughs when he sees me. He twirls a piece of his hair around his first finger, then uses the other hand to hug me. "What took you so long?" he asks, and I shrug, then tell him I had some stuff to take care of on earth. He nods like he understands, gets that serious look on his face that I know so well. It always makes me smile, even though I know I'm kidding myself. We'll never see each other again. Once you die, that's it, you're worm food. If there are other lives, it's not like anyone's got the courtesy to come back and tell you.

I see this homeless guy at the corner of Queen and McCaul. I have no idea how old he is. He's got a beard and his hands are caked with grease. He's missing one of his front teeth, and when he talks he slurs. He tells me he just drank a bottle of Listerine because he couldn't afford the cheapest wine, and I don't say anything at first. Then I nod and say, "You're probably pickling your insides with it." And he shrugs, like he knows, but what are you going to do? And there's this look of understanding that passes between us for a second, that I see even though his eyes are glazed. Like, I get it, how it is to need to find something to hang on to. I know how it is to feel like you have nothing. How a second of joy is worth any future pain on a day that is otherwise so dismal and mundane and just plain shitty that you just want to kill yourself. I get it, I really do. Talking to homeless people kind of cheers me up. More than anything, I like the human contact. And I like knowing that it could always be worse.

I check my bank account. There's exactly $3.12 in it but, of course, I have overdraft facilities to keep me alive. I take out a twenty, crumple it and shove it into my wallet, along-side a thousand receipts and old photos and business cards I no longer remember getting.

I recently quit a job in a restaurant. I was bussing, waiting tables, and washing dishes one day in a Queen Street greasy spoon when I realized how pointless it was. It was a revela-tion that had been building for weeks but hit me in the gut that day like a bag of bricks. I don't even know what caused it, but I know it was all I felt until I couldn't feel anything else or stand to work there anymore. My hands were always cold and raw, and the customers were jackasses who never tipped enough. I was barely getting by, barely paying rent, and I was full of this aching, never-leaving sense that I could do better. I have this feeling buried deep in my gut that I was meant to do more with my life.

HE BELIEVED I WAS SPECIAL. WHEN WE WERE TOGETHER, HE made enough money that I didn't have to work. I was an art student, and I was kind of appalled at myself, shocked that I didn't care about taking his money. It's just that I was com-fortable; I was so completely sure that he loved me that I didn't stop to feel guilty, or wonder how I'd support myself without him.

He was a photographer—he shot musicians and actors and other famous people. He travelled to LA sometimes, and to New York, but he did a lot of his work in studios in Toronto. Our basement had its own darkroom and was full of cameras—old and new. He wasn't afraid to embrace digital, but he loved the old stuff too. Sometimes he talked, full of passion and life, tried to bring me in, played with my hair, showed me examples, and I didn't always get it, but I wanted to. I always wanted to try.

Sometimes I travelled with him. We were in San Francisco one July when we met Astrid. She was a photographer too, and divorced. She was a year younger than him, compared to my eleven years. She was lean, with thin arms and well-defined cheekbones. She had blond hair and didn't shave her underarms. She made me feel vain and girly, unsophisticated and unworldly. She made me feel like she was the kind of woman he'd want to be with, the kind he deserved.

Maybe my fears became a self-fulfilling prophecy. I believed them, and started holding back, moving away from him, disconnecting. We hadn't made love in two months when he told me. He cried and sat on the edge of the bed and told me that it happened once, and that it hadn't meant anything. But I knew it had. I knew he was lying.

Our fights were messy. He put his knee through one of my canvases and I smashed a couple of his cameras, threw one out the window, another down a flight of stairs. I could see her when I looked into his eyes. I found blond hairs in his suitcase. I felt like I could smell her on his fingers. I couldn't get it out of my head.

SIX MONTHS AFTER WE BROKE UP, AFTER ASTRID STOPPED calling and went back to her husband, he started using again. He never said it, but I knew it was true. I was as sure he was doing heroin as I was of my own name.

I visited him a couple of times after I moved out—a month later and two months after that. It didn't look like our house anymore. All the blinds were drawn, and tin foil covered the bathroom window. The kitchen cabinets were full of huge cases of it—more tin foil than I'd seen in my life. There wasn't a single ray of light, except for the dull sheen of the TV. He'd stare blankly at it, not seeing anything. His eyes glazed over when he looked at me. I'd find half-eaten tins of SpaghettiOs with forks in them on the kitchen counter, an unflushed toilet in the bathroom.

He was running out of money all the time and kept asking me for more. When I said no, he'd have the kind of volatile mood swings you read about in books. I didn't want to be his mother, I didn't want to have to control him. He was supposed to be the older one, he was supposed to know what to do. I didn't have a fucking clue. I cried so much at night all my pillows were stained with mascara. As far as I knew, rehab cost money, which neither of us had.

I didn't know how to save a grown man, where to begin. He obviously didn't want me around, didn't want to hear anything I had to say. If I was excited about something he'd answer sarcastically, without any interest. I tried to kid around with him, lighten up when I saw he didn't like it when I was serious. I brought *Family Guy* DVDs and cheap red wine. I'd run my fingers over his track marks and he'd purr like a cat getting its chin scratched. We'd stare at the TV, laugh at all the dumb, obvious jokes. Sometimes his eyes would focus on me for a second, and things would feel normal. But it was over, and I knew it. I couldn't trust him.

WHEN HE DECIDED TO MOVE TO LONDON TO FOCUS ON HIS career I was relieved. Maybe he'd have a chance, maybe he could start a new life.

I wanted to be happy for him when he finished a rehab program there, but I was angry. I felt abandoned. I wasn't sure that I had ever been in love with him, not like in fairy tales with shaking knees and constant desire, but he'd been the most dependable companion I'd ever known, the kind that called me on my shit when I was wrong and treated me lovingly when I was good.

I didn't know how to function without him. I considered moving there, I considered visiting him. I didn't know what to do, until he called one day and gave me the news. He'd been feeling sick, so he went to a doctor to check it out. He had Hepatitis C. He probably got it years ago, but it can lie dormant in the body for years.

"Why did I bother getting clean?" he joked. "Think of how much drugs I missed out on."

He was lucky I was too far away to slap him.

He would call me from the hospital every day to tell me

how he was feeling. I booked a trip to London but didn't make it in time. He died two weeks before I was supposed to get there. An ex-girlfriend of his called to tell me, and we both cried.

I WALK TO YONGE AND QUEEN AND FIND A TAXI. THE TWENTY dollars is just enough. The driver takes me to the bridge that overlooks the Danforth. I have his stuff in the backpack I always take walking with me. A Jesus and Mary Chain album. A Cure single. A button-down shirt that stopped smelling like him a long time ago. Negatives that he never developed. A small point-and-shoot camera that he used when he walked down the street, to get ideas. I hurl the whole backpack over the edge. It hits the road below with a tiny thud. I have $1.75 left in my wallet. I watch as the sun starts to come out. It's 5 a.m. I've cried so much I can't even see straight. I have to walk home, and from here it might take two hours. I turn my back and start walking away.

I guess I have to start moving.

DON'T TALK JUNK

★

I CAN FEEL MY TEETH CRACKING IN MY HEAD. COMING DOWN is like that—it makes you feel every sensation in your body more intensely.

Last night we were lying in bed, and I found a big fat vein in between my thigh and my crotch. Actually, he found it— he was running his hands over my panties for the first time in months. I felt his nail run along a strip of raised skin— I felt a shiver somewhere in my neck, and I had to look down—it was purple and thick. It was better than sex. It was better than him on top of me, inside me, looking me in the eye, 'cause at that moment I couldn't even remember what colour his eyes were. The brush of someone's lips against yours or the sliding of someone's tongue doesn't compare with the smoothness of a needle. It's sharper, more real. It doesn't lend itself to any doubts.

I've been grinding my jaw for half an hour now and I can feel the enamel coming off the backs of my teeth.

He calls me at 1:35 in the afternoon. The flashing numbers of the call display are bright red against the

Christmas-green of my alarm clock. I pick up the phone and whisper into it. He asks me how I'm feeling. His voice is ragged. I tell him I'm thinking of taking the frozen peas out of the fridge and rubbing them against my jaw. I don't have an ice pack. He tells me he can't believe I'm living alone after all of this. I nod my head. I know. I can't believe it either. He asks me if I want to go to the park, between my apartment and his. He can get a dealer there in fifteen minutes. I drag myself out of bed, splash water on my face. When I look in the mirror, I notice that I still have the mark on my neck.

I can still see his teeth marks.

Before, when I had friends who weren't constantly fucked up, when I was still in school, this girl would tease me about not having any foundation or concealer. She'd say, "Angela has eye glitter in every colour of the rainbow but nothing to cover up a zit." I pick up a bottle of red sparkles and sprinkle them on my lips. I hit the top of my mouth on a door knob last night, and it looks like I've had a collagen injection. I am freezing. My body temperature is all fucked up now.

I live beside a park where fifteen-years-olds deal acid and shrooms, and I live in a building where a lot of people smoke crack. The elevators constantly smell like burning plastic. I never got into the rock, even though he does it, 'cause I believe you get what you pay for. My father used to say when you buy something cheap in life, there are always consequences.

None of the crackheads I know can function. None of them have jobs anymore, none of them are artists, half of them steal and do crazy shit just to get by. Crack is where I draw the line. I'm a lot of things, but I'm not a junkie.

I WAS REALLY YOUNG WHEN I MET HIM. IT WAS AT A PARTY— one of those fake-ID, looking-the-bouncer-in-the-eye, wearing-a-low-cut-shirt type of deals. He had a swagger— the kind of man who walked into a room and owned it. Every woman in the room was watching him.

I sat in the corner by the bar, drawing in my sketchbook with a thick black Sharpie. I was writing out my name in thick loopy letters, trying to come up with a tag. I wanted to start doing graffiti. I hated art school. I was sick of seeking approval from teachers who didn't think my work was technically good enough.

I wanted to professionally vandalize.

He came over to me and started talking. He said something about my Converse, about how pretentious the place was, how he could tell I wasn't like everyone else based on my shoes. He could have been with anyone, but he picked me. We shared a cigarette outside. I felt we connected, that he might understand me.

That night he took me back to his place. I wrote the letters of my name all over his arms and legs. I marked my territory. I sunk my teeth into his body.

He laughed and looked at me. "Are you trying to give me

a hickey? Want me to find a parking lot, and we can make out like sixteen year olds?"

I laughed too. "Yeah, I'd like that," I told him, and I wasn't sure if I was being sarcastic or not. In the dark, he traced the smile that crept to the tops of my cheeks.

I moved in with him two weeks later.

I'D NEVER LIVED WITH ANYONE EXCEPT MY MOTHER. SHE WAS a single mom, and for the longest time it was just me, her, and my youngest brother. My older brother moved out when I was twelve and got in trouble with the law. We're not allowed to talk about him. It's the Stern family way, or something. He dropped out of high school when he was sixteen, served some time in juvie, and now works at a gas station about twenty-five minutes away.

We don't talk about my father either.

My mother had a boyfriend for a while, this guy Steven. I liked him okay, I guess. He seemed like he was nice to her, and he was decent to me. He never told me what to do or how to live my life. She got pregnant and they seemed happy about it. Then one day, when my younger brother was three, he up and left her. They had never gotten married. My mother went crazy after that—yelling, screaming, blaming. She resented my little brother for standing in her way of being able to work full-time, and she resented both of us for putting her in a position where she had to work full-time. She was too proud to go on any kind of assistance, so for months at a time we subsisted on macaroni and cheese and Cheerios. When we were good we got McDonald's.

My mother alternated between screaming at me for not being more maternal, not wanting to be a mother to my little brother, and confiding in me about our finances, her job, and her loneliness. On the one hand, she insulted me so much it was crippling; on the other, she wanted to be my best friend. She got me a cellphone, and would call me during the day, complaining about me and whatever was wrong with her life. She never developed the skills to communicate that she was having a bad day—I began to understand that when she said terrible, insulting things to me, she was simply stressed.

At the same time, I was fifteen and I had angst of my own. I was an average student at best, despite her expectations. I hated school: I hated the people, I hated the curriculum. My mother was Jewish and killed herself to send me to a private Jewish high school. She never bothered to ask me whether I wanted to go there or not, and I doubt very much that she would have cared if I'd given her my answer. My mother was one of those people—it was her way or the highway. After high school and spending two years sleeping on people's floors and couches, in basements, and in the hallways of strangers, I finally chose the highway. He helped me find it.

It wasn't that difficult leaving her. My mother had been making my life a living hell for years. He never liked hearing about how my mother and I didn't get along. His mother died when he was young, and they'd been close.

"It's a tragedy," he'd tell me when he was pacing and sweating, needing a fix while I lay on the couch, with my legs splayed open, trying to find a new vein.

I'd look at him, accusatory. "I'm lying here like this, and you don't even want me," I'd spit.

"Oh, for fuck's sake, Angela," he'd scream, and throw a beer bottle against the wall above my head. It would narrowly miss me, and I'd be so caught up in what I was doing I'd forget to wince. That's what was happening to us. We couldn't even get a reaction from each other anymore.

"I'm going to find someone to fuck who'll give me more of their junk," he'd snap, finally.

He meant it too. He always meant it when he said things like that. It would dawn on me, hours later, when I realized where he was, when the feeling in my body and brain had returned. He'd crawl into bed, or beside me on the couch, at three or four in the morning, smelling like weed and perfume, with new rips in his jeans and fresh bruises everywhere. Sometimes his neck would ooze blood.

"Take care of me," he'd whisper, and I'd press my lips to his cuts. I'd rub my lower lip on his jagged edges and will the pain to go away. I could still feel his pain even if I couldn't feel my own. When I had the energy, I'd get up, go to the bathroom, find the disinfectant, and clean him off. When I was sure he had passed out, I'd cry. I'd wake up the next day with eyes so puffy it would take me ten minutes to be able to see.

WHEN WE MET HE WAS A RECORD PRODUCER, AN UP-AND-coming success story. He'd always dreamed of working at a major label, he told me three nights after I moved in, and he was finally doing it. His voice sounded like a little boy's on Christmas morning. His enthusiasm was contagious. I started to believe I could do stuff with my life too. I started to think maybe I could be an artist, or a graphic designer, or work in advertising. We'd been to a party the night before where a tall, thin blond woman who worked in advertising had hit on him. I wanted to seem worldly and sophisticated like her.

I got a job as a secretary in the office of a music publisher friend of his. He was doing lines of coke in the office bathroom and he slapped my ass and offered me the job, telling me that his last girl had just quit. I wasn't afraid of him—I didn't think he'd actually come on to me, knowing that I was with Paul.

There are so many fringe benefits to doing drugs. When Paul and I started going out, he taught me some tricks to keeping the weight off. Coke helps a lot, but heroin is fantastic. Being an addict is way cooler to most people than being overweight. I was never exactly what you would consider fat, but I was definitely voluptuous. Having big breasts as a sixteen-year-old is entirely overrated. You get the wrong kind of attention—you know, gawking guys in the 7-Eleven when you're buying a Slurpee—but never the love and respect that you want from the guy you like. I'd show up to grade ten English in a low cut maroon tank top and my crush would never look my way. I knew what my mother would tell me. She'd tell me it was because I was fat. "That's the way the world works," she would say. "I didn't make the rules."

Paul was the first person to make me feel like she was wrong. He was the first person to make me feel like I could do more with myself, like I could have the life I always wanted. He gave me so many ways to escape.

I would have done anything to make him happy.

"WE SHOULD GO OUT MORE," I'D SOMETIMES SAY, STARING AT the tiny strip of light between the curtains. "We haven't left the house in days."

Sometimes he'd make me fake promises in a lilting, romantic voice. He'd wrap his arms around my waist, and sweep me up. He'd whisper things, press his nose into the side of my face. I'd feel the tension draining out of my body. I'd feel myself collapsing into him.

Other times, he had no patience, and he'd tell me if I wanted to go out I could make a run for our next stash. I'd move weakly toward the door, hoping to be able to get him whatever he needed to be happy again. I never knew how to make him happy, aside from bringing him chemicals.

About two weeks after I moved in, I found him chopping some crystal meth on a mirror in the bathroom. I stood by the sink, staring, then snorted some as he sat on the toilet beside me, shuddering and breathing in. It made the anxiety go away. It chopped my guilt into thin lines that floated away. We'd do it every night at six, when he got home from the studio. The first time I went out to get us more he looked at me with so much pride. I had to turn my back so he wouldn't see how emotional I was. Trying to get another reaction like that from him was how I got through the days sometimes. I avoided the mirror on my way out for fear of what I might look like to other people, to people who didn't use.

He'd get that look on his face, that desperation in his eyes, that "I would kill my own mother to get a hit" look. And when he got his five or so grams, magic would cloud his irises and I could see the fireworks. I could see every colour he was seeing, feel every surge of energy that crept through his bloodstream. *It's love*, I told myself. *I know everything he's feeling at this moment because I love him.*

"Don't talk junk," he drawled in his South African accent, pushing the thought away with his thin, bleeding arm, when I told him.

"We don't have to talk about it," I'd tell him.

We don't have to talk about junk because I know what it's like. We don't have to talk about anything. I know.

When he was with it enough to tease me, he would. "Oh, I forgot," he'd say, trying to focus his line of vision on me. "You know everything."

I'd nod and rest my head on his shoulder, and he'd run his thin fingers through the hair I hadn't washed for days.

WE MEET AT THE PARK TO TALK. IT'S BEEN A FEW WEEKS SINCE we've done this properly, since we've really made time to speak. He used to love doing deals in the playground, by the sandbox, beside the jungle gym. I loved it too—it made me feel bad. We see someone dressed like Big Bird. There are a bunch of kids crowded around him, pulling at his feathers.

Paul leans in to me and whispers, "You know some people are into that."

I look at him. "Into what?"

"Wearing animal suits. They show up at your house or wherever, wearing one of these things, with a hole in the crotch."

I shake my head. I think he's making it up.

"No it's true," he insists. "Some people have weird fetishes. Some people are way weirder than us. Some people are way more fucked up."

I start to laugh. I remember why I love him. I tell him so, right then. I sprawl out on the bench, and put my legs up on him.

He strokes my left leg, close to my thigh.

I pat my belly. I tell him that things have to change. I'd told him that something terrible had happened, something that I didn't know how to deal with. We hadn't been living together for two months, but he could hear how freaked out I was on the phone. I'd told him that I couldn't do it alone, that I needed him, and I thought he understood, but now I'm suddenly less sure.

I say it in three words, and we sit in silence.

He turns his back to me, looks away, then turns to face me, looking me in the eye. I feel something stirring within me. A smile breaks out over his face. I'm so relieved I could vomit. I trace his smile with my index finger, and cast a shadow over the scars on his neck.

Coming clean was possible. Maybe a future is possible.

We both stare ahead, into the distance.

SMACKED

★

COLOUR EXPLODES OUT OF THE CORNERS OF MY EYELIDS. When I close my eyes, when things are supposed to be pitch black, I see it. Dancing fireworks, exploding paint cans, multi-coloured moving comforters and pillows.

She said it would go away if I just kept my eyes shut, put my head down. She promised that if I just tried to relax the frog feeling would go away. I feel like I have a frog hopping up and down in the middle of my brain, up and down, trying to get out. *Ribbet, ribbet.* Thick, gooey frog feet jumping in my skull. A warning sign: *Hello girl, you are way too smacked.*

As if I didn't know that already. As if I needed reminding.Thanks, brain, and partnership for a drug-free America, and after-school specials. Thanks. Now even my trips are unimaginative. Fuck the media and advertising for crushing my ability to space out interestingly, or just fucking relax. I wanted to paint or write, or something, and all I can think of are those stupid words cascading around some dumb flower—part of a *Don't Do Drugs* ad in a magazine I just opened: *You'll never have a high as good as your first, but feel free to die trying.* I wish I hadn't just seen that. Nothing like guilt to fuck up a perfectly good, perfectly expensive trip.

My dealer is the first South African I've met in ages. I tap the magazine with my chipping pink nails and look up at her. She stares blankly for a second, then it registers. *"Ai tog,"* she murmurs, then shrugs.

I feel the spit gathering in the sides of my mouth. My tongue feels fuzzy. *"Jirre fok,"* I say, surprised at how angry I am. Fuck God. I love swearing in Afrikaans.

"What are you planning to do for the rest of the night," she asks me suddenly, in English. English can sound so abrupt, so to-the-point.

"Nothing," I tell her, not looking up.

"I have to go," she says, getting up. One long graceful movement. She used to be a dancer. *"Vat dit rustig,"* she says. Take it easy.

I always do, and she knows it. *"Moerse fokken rustig*, I tell her, smiling. Majorly fucking easy. I never had any other intentions.

MY DEALER IS A GIRL I'VE KNOWN MY WHOLE LIFE. WE WENT TO the same Afrikaans hippie art school, and even had some of the same friends. The school was so small that everyone kind of knew everyone else. My sister was friends with her sister so, naturally, we hung out at each other's houses as kids. I don't have a lot of specific memories of her, except that when our mothers made us do ballet together, she enjoyed it. I, on the other hand, made every excuse to get out of it. I always had a hard time with instructions, with being told what to do, with having to follow someone else down to the letter.

She had this perfect, slender dancer's build; her body was like clay the teacher could mold into whatever image she felt like. I kind of hated her for it. My mom once asked me why I couldn't be more like that Suzette girl, which may have also had something to do with it. She was beautiful: naturally blond, makeup-free even in high school, with those tiny proportions and delicate feminine laugh. Guys loved her. I mean, it's not like I was exactly ugly, but next to her I felt like a giant with clumsy, klutzy gestures, tripping on my words and my feet. She was nice, sharp, and funny, but after grade ten we lost touch.

She got accepted into some American ballet school, and my friends and I went to different South African universities and studied various kinds of fine arts. Almost every one of my friends went into graphic design so, to be different, I became a copywriter.

I know what people say about advertising, about how evil it is, about capitalism and selling people crap they don't need and all that, and you know what? I don't disagree. But what else am I supposed to do, you know? Aside from design and advertising, what else can you do with a fine arts degree?

I'm a cliché in a lot of ways, I know it. I go to indie rock shows at the age of twenty-four. I try to keep up with what's cool. I wear skinny jeans and Ramones T-shirts. I make up stupid slogans during the day and drink with people at night. The thing is, I got bored of the South African scene. You hit the ceiling there really fast, in terms of living the artist's life. You meet everyone, sleep with everyone, go to festivals like Oppikoppi and Grahamstown one too many times, and that's it. Plus, everyone who's Afrikaans in the arts knows everyone else. It's always *ken jy vir*, fill in the blank: Do you know/have you gone out with/have you slept with/did your sister go to school with _____? And the answer is inevitably yes.

I got bored. I mean, I know there's a lot to be said for sticking to one's own culture and all that, and unlike a lot of my friends, I'm actually not a self-loathing Afrikaner. I've never understood people who hate their own culture. Why hate what you can't possibly change? The past and the actions of people who died before we were born aren't any more in our control than anything else. Why waste the energy? I don't buy the myth that we've completely changed as a culture, that we're so revolutionary now, but I do think we've gotten better. I do think our counterculture kicks ass, and so does our music scene. But still, it's a little too insular for me, you know?

So I decided to leave SA and move to the States. But I thought it would be easier than it actually was. I mean, getting a work visa was one thing, and so was getting a job. It took a few months, but I managed. I got a job in New York City, as a junior copywriter. If I'd stayed in SA a few more months I might have gotten a raise, possibly even a fancier title, like senior copywriter or something. I'd gotten my job straight out of varsity, was good at it, and liked it. I hear that's rare.

My mom was always talking to me about the crime though, ripping stories out of the newspapers and making me read them. She was thrilled when I told her I was leaving South Africa, so I figured it was a worthy investment. We were never that close—that is, until I left. Then she started calling me every night, long distance, just to see how I was, how I was doing in the big city. She worried about my English, if people understood me with my accent, if I was wearing my weird clothes to work, and if I was making any friends.

The truth is, I was running out of fabulous lies to tell her about my amazing lifestyle. I'd found an apartment in the East Village—sharing with a friend of a friend of my sister's. She was nice, but she had a boyfriend and they were never around. I mean, as far as living with a couple goes, it really wasn't as bad as it could have been. They didn't fuck loudly while I was in the living room or walk around naked or act lovey-dovey in front of me. They were just—barely there, the only signs were their underwear on the line on the balcony or their cigarette butts in the ashtray. The fridge was always empty, but she paid the cable bills, so there was always free TV. I'd never been a big TV watcher back home, but now I watched hours and hours of reality shows: *American Idol*, *Survivor*, and all the MTV shows about sweet sixteens. The daytime soaps made me homesick—I'd think about how much better South African soaps like *Egoli* or *7 De Laan* were, how they were more quality somehow.

The people at work barely spoke to me. I mean, they were loud and outgoing, everything I expected Americans to be, but when the clock hit five, they were out of there. No one stayed late, and no one said much to me except "Have a nice day," or "Take care." No one invited me to go for drinks or to chill. Guys didn't hit on me. I'd heard New York was great for its club scene, for its music and film and arts, but I didn't want to venture out on my own.

The thing about New York is that, in some ways, it's exactly what you expect. The buildings are huge and grey and make you feel overwhelmed. There are too many museums and restaurants to check out in one lifetime, even if you do have a huge social life. The sidewalks are always filled with people, too many to notice or even keep track of. I always think a person could disappear, and no one would ever know. It's grey and treeless and cold in winter. I arrived in November, and I'd never been colder in my life. I had acquaintances, I had a liquor store near my house, I had natural sleeping pills from the health shop. I wasn't happy, but it could've been worse. It could always be worse, I told myself.

I BUMPED INTO SUZETTE AT A STARBUCKS. I WOULDN'T HAVE recognized her at first—she had long blood-red hair and a nose ring—but I smiled when I heard her accent. She was sitting on the patio, reading Milan Kundera's *Unbearable Lightness of Being* and telling a bunch of pigeons who were congregating by her feet to *voetsek*, scram.

"*Ag, kom aan*," I said. Pigeons are cool.

"Pigeons," she said, not looking up, sounding annoyed, "are nothing more than rats with wings." She looked up and studied my face. A smile broke out. "Melanie? Oh my God!"

I was so happy to see someone I knew I forgot all about everything. I forgot I was supposed to dislike her, I forgot I wanted to forge my own way out of SA, become independent.

"What the hell are you doing here?" I asked.

We sat for two hours and talked. She told me all about her life, being in a dance company, her boyfriend, her friends. She told me that she sometimes missed SA, but that her life was full, so she didn't think about it too much. I started to cry, telling her how lonely I was, how I must have been insane to leave all security behind, how challenges were stupid, how I must be such an idiot to think I could make it in a place like this.

She patted my back. "Come out with us tonight. It'll be okay." She wrote her number down on a napkin, along with her address and directions. "Call me at 11:30," she said. I'd gotten so used to being on my own, to not going out, that 11:30 on a Wednesday night seemed really late.

I called her and took a cab. We went to a club near her

house that was chill, very relaxed vibes. We played pool, had beer with her friends. We all went back to her house and watched a movie, something dark and depressing that I would've loved if I was in a better frame of mind.

"You know what your problem is?" she said after, studying me. "You're, like, closed, you're cold and unfriendly. People don't talk to you because you don't talk to them. You need, like, a lesson in social interaction."

Her comments stung.

"The thing is," she said to me, a little more kindly now, "it doesn't come naturally to all of us. It doesn't come naturally to me either." She reached into her bag and pulled out two MDMA pills. "This helps a lot. I should have given you some before the night started, but, like, I dunno, I thought you'd do a little better, I thought you'd be okay."

I looked at her incredulously. "You've got to be kidding me, Suzette. You've got to be fucking kidding me. I worked in fucking advertising for two years. You gotta do better than fucking MDMA." I checked her out now, gave her the same withering look that she'd given me. "Suzette, you're twenty-six, *ne*? There's no way you can be that thin without a little help."

She grinned. "God, Melanie, I never knew you and your friends were into that."

I rolled my eyes. "*Duidelik*," I said, trying to sound blasé. Obviously.

ONE OF THE BIGGEST PERKS OF ADVERTISING WAS THE COKE WE
got offered nearly constantly. We'd go to clients' houses for
dinner—kind of fancy events with three courses and expensive red wine—and for dessert there'd be a silver box in the
middle of the table, and we'd all get a pinch or two. The first
time I went to something like that I was twenty-two and a
little shocked. I mean, my friends and I smoked grass and
hash and things like that in varsity, and on occasion we did
mushrooms or MDMA, but nothing too serious or heavy. It
wasn't that I was scared, it was just that I hadn't done it or
even heard anything about it before. I didn't know what to
expect.

It didn't make me feel warm and fuzzy like MDMA, didn't
make me want to kiss or sleep with strangers, or make me
want to dance and paint and have a great time. It did make
me feel more confident, though, more powerful, as if I suddenly realized that what I had to say mattered, that despite
my youth, I was worthy of my job and salary. And it helped.
People started listening to what I had to say, started taking
me more seriously. The truth is, people become addicted
to drugs for a reason. Drugs are great. They bring you out
of yourself and make life more fun. A client started listing
cokeheads to me: people in broadcasting, actors, musicians,
radio and TV personalities. I can understand why, I really
can. It gives you confidence like nothing else.

Coke gives you stamina when you're tired, like five vodka
Red Bulls. My friend Michele and I used to joke that one

day we'd make an ad campaign marketing coke to college students.

"Think about all the finals and presentations that would be passed with flying colours," I'd say.

"Literally," she'd add.

We'd laugh. But seriously, what an easy sell. Talk about a product whose benefits far outweigh its negative side effects.

The thing is, being a cokehead is a serious problem for a lot of good reasons. I never wanted to become a cokehead, so I never used unless someone bought some for me. I refused on principle to buy any myself, or to have any dealer's phone numbers.

When I came to New York I had no clue how to find any dealers and, besides, I knew New York was different than SA. In SA there are so many bigger problems that few cops give a shit about drug deals. I've gone to so many clubs, just regular bars that don't look seedy at all but have people openly doing coke in the bathrooms, on pool tables, or on chairs in the back at midnight on a week night. But I knew in the US I couldn't afford legal troubles, and I wasn't an addict, I was just a person who used sometimes for fun or a career boost.

Still, I hadn't done any in three months. Suzette took some out of a cigarette case in her bag, one of those flat business-card holder type of things. What a genius invention. It was good stuff, better than any I'd done before.

"It's from Colombia," she said. "My friend Miguel brought some back." It turns out her friend Miguel is a film producer/dealer. Arty and well-connected.

"I think I've found my new circle," I told her. She was thrilled.

THE NEXT THREE WEEKS WERE A BLUR OF GOING OUT PARTYING at night and coming to work trying not to appear hungover. Suzette was my friend, but she was also my dealer. She charged me money after a while; I had never paid for it before, on principle, but I guessed that here I had no choice. Besides, she was South African, a girl I went to school with—I had to trust her. She always looked extra beautiful when she was high. The black circles would disappear from under her eyes, and they'd get this sparkle that I never saw otherwise. She'd sit yoga-style when she was about to do a line, focused, one long leg over the other. She'd tell me about some book she was reading; her friend Joanne, this hippie with long brown hair and lots of beaded necklaces, would talk about something Buddha or Krishna said, or something about being a vegetarian; and Miguel would look at me hungrily, his brown eyes shining like stones washed by the sea.

Nothing happened between him and me for weeks, and that's what made it even better when it finally did. He took me to see a Harmony Korine movie at an independent movie theatre near where I lived, and then he took me back to his apartment. We rode his motorcycle to get there, and it felt amazing. I was high, so I was hot and cold—the night air was freezing but my heart was racing. I gripped his waist, and he turned around, smoothed the hair out of my face. We did three or four more lines at his place, ordered Indian takeout at three in the morning, had great sex, and talked about life.

It was Miguel who turned me onto H. He told me it was better than coke, and he didn't lie. The first time we did it was one of the best days of my life. I can't remember ever feeling closer to anyone, ever feeling physically better, or more in touch with myself, or wanting to share anything like that with anyone else. He injected it into me with so much tenderness and love, I felt my veins vibrate. I never wanted to do it alone after that.

The side effects of my new lifestyle so far had been mostly great: I'd lost weight, was generally more efficient at work, had more friends and a boyfriend. My job was so mechanical a monkey could do it. I was getting the same pay, stumbling in, and no one cared, and still no one talked to me. They seemed relatively satisfied with my work. Whatever they gave me to do I still did, sometimes twice as fast if I was high and not hungover or craving anything.

True, I was spending a lot of my money on drugs, but it was better than spending my money on food, and Miguel took care of most other things. Suzette's friends made me feel like I was taking in culture; they'd talk about things that had substance instead of the insipid small talk people made at work.

"This is what I came to America for, you know?" I'd say to Miguel, late at night. I'd run my hands over his skinny hips, and trace his bones with my index finger.

"Of course," he'd say, with his thick accent. "Of courrrse."

MIGUEL AND I MOVED IN TOGETHER AND MADE PLANS TO TAKE a trip to South America that summer. Colombia and Chile. Mexico. I took a bunch of sick days. I lost touch with all my friends, including Suzette. I didn't need her anymore. She called and said she missed my company and wanted to visit. I thought she was full of shit but didn't say it.

"Her wallet misses you," Miguel said, and I nodded.

When she came she looked totally different, fuller figured, fatter. I almost didn't recognize her. Her skin and hair shone so much it hurt my eyes to look at her. She squinted in the semi darkness of our apartment and shook her head. Some kind of emotion registered in her eyes that I couldn't place.

"*God gee genaude,*" I think I heard her mutter. God have mercy.

She called me a junkie and it hurt more than anything. It felt like being smacked by my mother as a kid when she'd found out I cheated on a test in grade two. For some reason, it hurt more coming from Suzette than from anybody else.

HEROIN HEIGHTS

★

TODAY I ACTUALLY REMEMBER BEING IN SCHOOL. SO MANY DAYS have been a blur lately, but this afternoon stood out. We were learning about the body in biology. When the teacher asked about the kidneys and their function, I put up my hand.

Finally, something I knew.

"They're bean-shaped organs the size of my fist," I said. "There are two of them, they're reddish brown, and they're located in my upper abdomen. Their function is to filter waste, fluids, and extra salt out of my blood."

For once, my teacher was impressed with me. Then she asked me, and the class, what happens when kidney's fail. I stared at her blankly, like I didn't know, except that I did.

"You die," she said harshly, then moved on to the pancreas.

I guess it takes hearing it from someone completely ob-jective, someone who's just stating the facts. Someone who doesn't know it's you. It was like a reminder, a loud alarm clock telling me my organs are rotting. My kidneys are failing.

It feels like I'm being kicked hard and fast by someone wearing soccer cleats. It feels like I'm not in control of my own body. I have to watch as it ejects food and swells up like a balloon. My eyes get puffy and I feel my body temperature drop by, like, a million degrees. Everyone who knows is worried about me, which just makes me feel guilty. They keep telling me I'm going to dehydrate.

It's been raining a lot, and sometimes I wish I could lie down outside, on the pavement, with my mouth open, drinking it all. I wish getting better were that easy.

The doctors have made it clear to my mom that I need more dialysis. I've had this condition since I was eight, but it got a lot more serious this year. The thing I know for sure is, we can't afford it, even though my mom denies it. She shouldn't—I'm too old, I know the truth.

"I got no more *ubuqwebe*," my mother yelled at no one in particular this morning. She had no more jewellery left to hawk. We're officially *skepselas*, the poor folk. Not that we were ever exactly fat cats, but we managed. My mom used to make more money, and she used to have a boyfriend who lived with us and helped out. Now it's just the two of us. Now we have to do embarrassing things, like show up at the hospital and beg. Half the hospitals around here won't even look at you if you don't have a gunshot wound, if you're not dying on the spot.

"You should *jola* one of the doctors, Mom," I joke as we sit in the taxi on our way to the hospital. "You're still good-looking, you could make it happen."

"*Uyabeda*," she spits at me, disgusted. "You're talking garbage. What, you think I'm a *magosha* now?"

It's the first time I've seen her look really angry in months. It kind of feels good, almost normal.

It's raining as we get out of the two-Rand taxi—a Zola Budd, as they say around here—a Toyota, which is missing its windows and its licence plate. It's a four-four, where you sit with four people next to you on each side, and the kid sitting next to me, who was probably five with sticky hands, kept grabbing at my hair. I had to control the urge to bite her.

It's 9:30 at night, forty-five minutes after my mom got off work, at the nearest hospital fifteen minutes from our flat. It's Hillbrow Hospital, the H Hosi, as they call it around here. We walk past a park and a school, plus a bunch of day-care centres. I guess all the teenage mothers and gang members have to put their kids somewhere. My mom thinks this side of Hillbrow is a lot safer than where we live, but I'm not so sure. I was kicking one of those small Coke cans as we walked into the hospital and I nearly stepped on a syringe. It could've gone right through my shoe, but I kept my mouth shut. She's got enough shit to worry about as it is.

We live in Highpoint, which actually is a physically high point, on a hill, right in the middle of Hillbrow. If the *tsotsis*, the thugs that hang out outside our building smoking all the time are right, our area is the number one place for drug deals in South Africa. They call it Heroin Heights, but what I've seen a lot of is crack and coke.

The streets are lined with one-star hotels, street meat vendors, and *magoshas* getting ready to *hlahla* any guy desperate enough to pay them. Our apartment is on Claim Street, near Kotze, across the road from the infamous Protea Hotel. It's legendary for the number of *jijis*, underage girls, that are there all the time. I can see them from my window without squinting. Sometimes there are moms, like in their forties even. I can see it in the lines in their faces, that dead look in their eyes. They stand outside, smoking *dagga*, staring vacantly into the street. At night the prostitutes are way younger. Some of them look my age. They all wear the same gold or purple eyeshadow, red lipstick, and black fishnets or torn tights. When their legs are bare you can see bruises and sometimes scratches. When they bend over, you can see everything. No underwear.

Every night when I go to bed my room is bathed in orange and green neon from the hotel sign. One of my mom's friends once offered to make me some curtains, but I said no. Orange and green are my favourite colours.

My mom is taking control of the situation at the hospital now. My legs feel like they're going to buckle any second. She's got this hard look in her eyes, this street look I've seen her use with the guy who drives the banana-*kaar* through our street. He comes by once a week, exchanging our used bottles for bags of popcorn and chips. We spend hours scrounging for stuff, swiping liquor bottles from our neighbours' garbage. Then he tries to stiff us, tries to give us half, or less, of the amount he owes us. Then my mom goes from being friendly and polite, a *mam'gobozi* who gossips with him, to his worst enemy. There's this moment of disbelief, this palpable look of shock on his face, before he just gives up and gives her what she wants. My *ouledi* is badass.

My eyes begin to well up and I wonder if she notices. A while ago I learned how to cry in public without anyone noticing. I don't change my facial expression, and I let the tears fall individually. I think being quiet is the best way to get away with anything. A couple years ago, I got bullied by some kids at school. I once got pushed in front of a door and everyone laughed as it slammed in my face. My lip was swollen and the skin above my nose and under my eyes bulged into hard red bumps. I sat crouching behind the door, bleary eyed and blubbering in pain. No one came near me or said a word. Guys walked right past me, and this girl that I thought was cool and wanted to be friends with saw me, laughed, and kept walking. I haven't been able to cry in public since.

My mom knows me better than anyone. She can tell I'm about to break down, so she steers me past the front desk. She finds a single empty chair, and I sink into it. It's made of worn blue leather and has stuffing coming out of its right arm. There's a table full of dog-eared magazines beside me. I leaf through an old issue of *Time*, feel disgusted, put it down.

My mom leans against the side of my chair. There's nowhere for her to sit. She works harder than anyone I know. The best word for it is *phithezela*—hectic. She cleans houses six days a week. When I get up in the morning she's already gone, and when I get home she's still not back yet. She's hardly ever around, so she can't take care of me when I'm sick. I don't want her to feel bad about anything. I understand that she needs to work.

"It could be a lot worse," I say. "We could be out on the street."

She shakes her head and looks away. "Aiiii," she mutters, shaking her head. "We nearly there, hey."

We haven't had electricity for three days now. It's fine during the day, but at night I have to use a torch just to get to the bathroom. I can't see to do my homework or read, I can't listen to music, and my boyfriend can't even call me.

My boyfriend is from Zimbabwe. His name is Munya. He's one of the refugees who hopped the fence, walked, crawled, climbed, and possibly killed to get into this country. He's eight years older than me. He's six feet tall, and thin. I can feel his hip bones and his rib bones when I touch him. He's gentle, at least he is with me. He's different than most guys I've met.

If my mom thinks anything bad about him, she doesn't say. She knows he's older, but she thinks he's twenty, not twenty-five. She was happy when he got a job in computers, so when he got fired last month, I didn't tell her. When he takes me out, she doesn't need to know where he gets his money.

It's hard to meet a guy around here who doesn't deal drugs. Munya doesn't *gufa*—he doesn't smoke crack or do coke. He just deals it because it moves a lot faster than weed, and he makes so much money that if he gets caught he'll be able to pay his bail. It's not so bad when you think about it. He doesn't see *magoshas* or have *phamakote*, AIDS.

We have sex, and most of the time we use condoms. It's hard to remember all the time. When passion grabs you, it grabs you, it's something intangible, a force that you can't control. It's a feeling I've always wanted to feel, so if it seizes me I try not to say no. Sex helps the world go black, it makes me forget that I'm sick, that I could die, that we have no money, that I might make nothing of my life. There's a gnawing fear in me that I'm not as good as my classmates, that I can try and struggle and still not end up like them—with two parents, a nice house, money, security, maybe a husband and kids one day.

I can't tell my mom that I'm having sex. She'll think that I *malunde*, that I sleep around. She'll be scared of me getting pregnant. Most of all, she's scared I'll never be a *makoti*, a bride. She's scared I'll end up tainted, used and thrown away like her. She wants everything to be better for me than it was for her. Sometimes it feels like too much to promise her.

She strokes my hair now. I used to wear it in tight, thin braids to make it feel like I had extensions. I felt so weird about having hair that's red and soft to the touch and grows at such a tremendous rate. I guess I've gotten used to it now.

She starts filling out the hospital forms for me. She writes out my date of birth and then my age. I'm going to be seventeen next week. It'll be at least a couple of hours before anyone can see us. I close my eyes. I wish I had something to knock me out. I open my eyes and find my mom filling out her section. Occupation: Housekeeper. Nanny. Professional Taker of Other People's Shit. She gets down on her hands and knees and scrubs their floors for less than a thousand rand a month. She makes them huge meals with fancy food, and we're subsisting on Fruit Loops with milk that's past its expiry date. They treat her like a *sbotho*, a worthless person they can replace any time. Which I guess they can. My mom has a grade-five education. When I graduate from high school, it'll be a big deal to her.

When I look around me sometimes, when I think about my chances of making anything of my life, I get incredibly depressed. I don't know what I want to be, or what I want to do, except make a lot of money. Enough to buy us a house. Enough to get my mom some nice new things. Enough for decent food. I keep telling my mom that if I eat any more *achaar*, which is township salad, oily, made of mangoes, that I'll be *sika* for the rest of my life. I keep telling her my kidney problems come from eating too much *achaar* and chicken dust, which is meat, any meat, it could be pigeon for all we know, sold by street vendors. Sometimes she laughs, but usually she snaps and tells me I'm being a *chizzboy*, a spoiled brat.

I like to fantasize about dropping out of school and being a singer or a rapper. I love *kwaito*, township hip hop, and African singers. My mom has all the albums, from Miriam Makeba to Brenda Fassie, from Bongo Maffin to Mandoza. *Kwaito* adds colour when everything is grey and white—the buildings; the crap burger joints; the wet laundry that hangs out of our windows, showing off our underwear, reminding the world that we're working class; the gunshots at night. It's too bad my father was white. I'm a *dushi*, a mixed-race kid. I'd never be accepted if I wanted to make music like that. As it is, the kids I know from around here call me Coconut: brown on the outside, white on the inside. They hate that I don't go with them to one of the shit schools in the township. I go to an almost all white school in Edenvale that takes me forever to get to. My name is Colleen, which they call me at school, but in Hillbrow everybody calls me Coco.

A nurse comes to call us into another waiting area. She asks my mom if I have *Magama Amathathu*, if I have AIDS. She asks because I'm thin, because I haven't been keeping anything down.

I'm about to snap, I'm about to say, "No, lady, not AIDS, just HIV." It's the kind of joke my mom wouldn't find funny.

"I don't want a *phalafala*," she tells me, sharply poking me in the leg.

It's true, I know. The last thing we need is a fiasco.

Sometimes when I think about being *sika*, about how many years I've had these health problems, about how little money we have, how my mom has to *phanda*, try to make ends meet, I get so angry. I understand why people deal drugs, why people rob houses, why stupid people get shot. Everyone is desperate to get out of this place as soon as they can. And there are so many of us.

When we get called to the doctor's rooms—finally—we're told that we have to pay. The doctor explains that not treating me could be fatal. We panic and talk, pace the passageway, and think. I suggest calling Munya for the money and my mom relents. She still thinks he's a stand-up guy with a real job, instead of a *lova*, an unemployed guy who deals drugs and knows all the lyrics on Brenda Fassie's *Memeza* album.

It's his drug money that pays for the dialysis. When he doesn't have enough, he and his friends break into houses. They say they never hurt anyone, just scare them until the job is done. There's something exciting about it, about taking life into your own hands, but there's something scary about it too. When I think about my mom going to work in a five-year-old uniform that's missing its middle button, with a rag tied around her head, stealing sugar from the pantry because she's afraid to ask for some for tea, going without a lunch so I can eat—I feel so sad and angry and guilty.

When Munya asks me again to go with him and his friends to housebreak tomorrow night I think I'll go with. I mean, there's the future I want for myself, and then there's the truth, the one I see every day. The grey buildings, the drugs, the pocket knife I carry in my sock. I might do my best and still never get out of here.

I have to try it once, just to know.

I have to figure out if something, anything, makes me feel less angry.

THE APPLE FALLS FAR
FROM THE TREE

★

WHEN I WAS A KID I ATE THE SAME THING FOR DINNER EVERY night. Fried sole, homemade chips, and half an avocado. I ate it on a tray propped up on my knees as I watched *She-Ra: Princess of Power* at six on M-Net. I ate with my hands, food falling onto my mud-stained knees, and then hitting my dirty *plakkies* before I managed to grab it off my shoes and eat it anyway. Dirt never seemed to make me sick, but watching me eat almost killed my parents. They were civilized city people whereas, clearly, in another life I'd been raised in a barn.

Eating all that oil and starch didn't catch up to me until I was about nine. My cheeks started looking like they were stuffed with cotton wool. I developed a *boep*—which was embarrassing, not in the least because my arms and legs remained skinny and my chest remained flat as a board. In a desperate attempt to flatten my belly, my parents sent me to one dance class after another, all with the same results: I'd get bored within ten minutes and either start making up my own dances or wander off. I'd try to kill time in the bathroom, or ask the teacher if I could use her phone. By the time I'd get back, class would be over. The teacher would be as relieved as I was.

She was heavier than me, and seemed to have long ago lost her passion for the art. Besides, hearing the words *arabesque* and *demi-plié* pronounced with a heavy Afrikaans accent really makes them lose something. It's kind of like hearing opera words like *aria* and *basso buffo* said with a Scottish burr. Even if you could understand what they were saying, why would you care? It was that unnatural.

I'll never forget the time my mom came to watch a ballet recital. I really thought she was going to kill me. Not only had I not mastered any feminine arts, but I looked bored and was utterly graceless. I tripped and fell. I didn't get one step right. She nearly cried from shame. I was sure I was going to get *bliksemed* the second I walked in my front door.

After that we tried modern, tap, and aerobics to equally little avail. The older I got, the more my mom took to weighing me and hiding the keys to the pantry so I couldn't snack when she wasn't looking. I stubbornly refused to stop eating chocolate, reasoning that a world without Caramello Bears was not a world worth living in. I had to be careful though; she sometimes checked my homework, and a chocolate-smudged page could mean only one thing. I had to get really good at covering my tracks.

Aerobics offended me the most. To the tune of "Itsy Bitsy

Teenie Weenie Yellow Polka Dot Bikini," and other atrocities that barely qualify as music, two chubby little girls, my friend Amanda and I, bopped along with a group of fat and anorexic women. We wore T-shirts and shorts, they wore leotards and sweatbands across their foreheads. I protested until I turned blue in the face. Kicked and screamed until my arms were covered in scratches from the sisal rugs in my bedroom that could have been used as instruments of torture, they were that rough.

I think it was my grandfather who suggested I simply play school sports. May God rest his soul. There were two more classes my parents forced me into, gymnastics and swimming, before they gave up entirely. After that, I played tennis and netball, at school. If my performance was noteworthy, it was only in that I didn't completely suck. I was merely passable, which for me was an achievement. I almost broke my tailbone doing long jump once. I broke my leg in three places riding my bike. Being active was just not for me, that much was clear. While my parents ran the Comrades Marathon, I watched *Egoli*, my favourite soap opera.

I had a few secrets back then. When I was six I decided I wanted to be famous. I'd watch *Zoobilee Zoo* over and over, learning the lines of the pink kangaroo. I wanted to be cute and on TV, like her. I'd stare at myself for hours in the mirror, imagining it. When I was a little older, I wanted to be a KTV presenter, then a soap star. I wanted the constant spotlight. I also had a crush on a boy in my class called Joshua, who was so clever that he'd skipped a grade and went around making smart-alecky comments. I named all my boy dolls after him, even though I was too shy to actually talk to him.

Sometimes I wondered what it would be like to be what my parents wanted me to be—thin, athletic, good at math, feminine, a candidate for all kinds of future success. Sometimes I wondered what it would be like—to naturally be who they wanted me to be, without ever even trying.

I wondered if I'd be happier.

JUST, QUIETLY, DO IT

★

IT'S A FUNNY THING ABOUT BEING THROWN DOWN THE STAIRS.

If you know how to position yourself, you won't even crack a rib. There's nothing worse than breaking a rib. You can't get a cast, and you sit around all day trying not to breathe too hard, knowing that everything you do is going to hurt.

It's all in how you land. I learned a long time ago that fighting it was useless—it would just make it worse for me later. I've learned to let the side of my face hit the hardwood, and let my arms hang so they cushion my sides. That way, when I hit the ground I don't feel it as much. I keep concealer in the bathroom to cover up the bruises, and it's usually a few days before they show, anyway.

Being yelled at is much worse. The things they say hurt for much longer than the bruises. They always go at it together. Usually my mom yells and my dad hits, but sometimes it's vice versa. My parents are a tag team with a great marriage. The problem is me, not them. I am their biggest disappointment. Sometimes it's my grades that get them started, or my

clothes, or my driving, but lately it's been the fact that I talk
back to them a lot.

MY NEIGHBOUR DRIVES ME TO SCHOOL IN THE MORNINGS. HE'S
one grade ahead of me, and he drives his mom's minivan.
It's grey and the paint is chipping. He thinks he looks cool,
and I don't tell him that he doesn't because he's one of my
best friends. We drive blasting music like Pearl Jam and the
Killjoys, so I guess he is kind of cool. We used to carpool,
but that was until he got his driver's licence last year. It let us
ditch the weirdos we used to have to drive with.

His name is Diego, and he's from Mexico. He's small,
about 5' 7", and skinny. He has light brown hair, beady dark
eyes, and a long pointy nose. My mother calls him Speedy
Gonzales, except I think he looks more like a rat than a
mouse. I call him Speedy when it's just him and me, and he
thinks it's because of his driving.

He comes with me when I take my dog for walks, even
though I know he sometimes wants to kick him. After, we
go to the convenience store on Marlee to buy his cigarettes,
which I sometimes smoke. I have an easier time getting cigarettes than he does, even though we're both underage. Lots
of things are easier if you're a girl. You just wear a low-cut
shirt and some lip gloss and you're money to guys, I swear
to God.

Diego has dated a couple of my friends. One of them fell
in love with him. She told us he gave her can't-eat-can't-sleep

syndrome. I didn't really understand why, but I was happy for them. She's shorter than him, practically pocket-sized, with a button nose and a cute smile. I think she's adorable, but apparently Diego didn't. Neither did Jason. His locker was next to hers. When I told him about the hook up, he shook his head. "She smells like sheep shit," he said.

When Diego broke up with her after a few weeks later she cried every day at lunch and called Bethany and me crying every night. She only stopped after she heard the song "Time of Your Life" by Green Day. "These lyrics are exactly what I'm going through," she said. "They make me feel less alone."

DIEGO AND ME TALK SHIT THE WHOLE WAY TO SCHOOL, WHICH this morning takes twenty-five minutes. He makes fun of my clothes and I make fun of his accent. He tells me his mom is making quesadillas tonight and I should come over and try them. My weight is a huge issue for my parents, so I'm happy to eat anywhere other than my own house. I say yes, then we start talking about music videos. This is massively distracting from what happened last night, so I'm really happy.

As soon I get to school, I make a beeline for Bethany's locker. Taped inside, she still has a poster of Leonardo DiCaprio from that movie *Romeo and Juliet* that I gave her in grade nine. We met in art class that year. She happened to be sitting beside me. Bethany has fine brown hair that she used to wear in baby barrettes with cutesy plastic cutouts on them of Elmo and other *Sesame Street* characters. I was taking the class because I loved it, but she was taking it because she was deathly afraid of performing in front of people, so that meant drama was out, and art was her only other choice. It was the one class where her incredible brain didn't shine—Bethany doesn't have one creative bone in her body. Otherwise, her grades are stellar—she gets straight A-pluses and wasn't about to let some stupid elective get in her way. She wants to go to an American Ivy League school like Harvard or Stanford.

Unlike her, my grades are painfully average. I mean, at a normal school Bs and Cs would be fine, but at the overachieving private school my parents forced me to go to, they are well below average. Art was the one class I liked, because I love painting more than anything. I didn't even mind doing Bethany's paintings, and she rewarded me with her friendship.

I really hate the girls we go to school with, with their $500 Kate Spade purses and flat-ironed hair. Bethany and I bonded over 80's kids shows, like *My Little Pony*, and being ditched by our best friends in junior high.

"Best friends are people who screw you over," Bethany told me one day, and I nodded in agreement.

We hung out all the time, took photos together, went shopping, wrote each other letters to read on the plane before one of us went on vacation, but we never called each other our best friend. It was an unspoken rule.

By grade ten, we were both fifteen and had never kissed a guy. We talked about our crushes on guys: she thought Tiger Woods had a nice ass; I liked the dude from Savage Garden because I thought he seemed sensitive. I went away to England that summer with my family and made a couple of new friends. One night, after hanging out with some people, a guy walked me home. He had a great accent and blond hair. He kissed me fast, and kind of wet, and even though it wasn't that great, it was a big deal and I knew it. When I got home, I called Bethany, and instead of being happy for me like I expected, she was disappointed.

"We were the same before, and now we're not," she said. "It's like you're better than me now, and you didn't used to be, and I'm not sure how I feel about that."

It was the beginning of the end for us. I mean, people still think we're really close, and we still act like we are. But things aren't the same, even if we're the only ones who know it.

After she asks me how I am, and we talk a little about last night's TV shows, we both have to go to class. At our school, they keep tabs on us all the time. It's freaky and Orwellian. We just read *1984* in English, so I know. Big Brother is watching you, all that stuff. If you're late they send you to an office downstairs where the attendance secretary signs a pink sheet of paper and writes the words "unexcused absence." If you fill up both sides of the paper before the end of the semester, you get suspended. Guess who's really, really close. Yep, I have only four lines to go.

I go to the bathroom, which makes me late, so I have to go downstairs. The attendance secretary calls my parents. My mother sounds eerily calm on speaker phone, so I know I'll be in real shit when I get home.

JASON, THE GUY I LIKE, IS IN MY GEOMETRY CLASS. I USED TO HATE geometry until I figured out that the De Stijl artists used it for their paintings. Now I don't love it, but I don't hate it as much. He says hi to me and touches my elbow on his way in. Now that he has a girlfriend, it's okay for him to be friendly to me in public. She goes to another school, a public school near where he lives. They see each other all the time. Her name is Sarah, and they knew each other when they were little kids. He bumped into her at a party. They started going together right away, even though he and I were still messing around at the time. Now we're just friends and we talk sometimes, but not that much. We don't hang out alone anymore. My friends seem to think it's for the best, even though it hurts me more than they know.

He wears the same thing every day: brown cords or khakis and a freshly ironed shirt with a small fancy logo sewn on the pocket. He wears a cologne called Minotaur that he got from his dad. It's hard to find, he told me, and expensive. He has wavy brown hair that spirals into perfect tight curls at the ends. He has a face like a little boy's, wide blue eyes with long lashes, and pale skin. He used to act surprised when I told him he was beautiful. "Do you think I'm handsome?" he asked me once, dissolving into laughter when I said yes.

When I first told Bethany that I liked him, she laughed and said that I had no chance with a guy like that. Which seems really mean, but it's kind of true. The girls he hangs out with are petite and cute, with amazing bodies and trendy clothes. Their clique is super tight, and he's the only guy they hang out with.

It's not that I'm not pretty, or smart, or whatever, it's just that I'm different from them. I wear hippie blouses I find in Kensington Market and baggy jeans, and the perfume I wear is called Grass and actually smells like a lawn. I get that people wouldn't think I'm his type.

We met in English class and bonded over books. We decided to work together on a presentation about song lyrics analysis. I was so excited I couldn't sleep the night before I had to go over to his house. When he held my hand I felt an electric ripple through my whole body. When he kissed me I was shocked, and so happy. I'd never felt like that before.

I called Bethany right away. I told her everything we talked about, everything he told me, after. How he didn't want a girlfriend right then. Maybe in the future, but not then. How he still wanted to mess around—like make out and stuff.

"Isn't this what we've always wanted?" I asked her. "Experience?" I said it all in one breath, so I had to stop.

She waited about a minute to respond. "I see no difference," she said, "between what you do and a prostitute. Face it, Katie, if you agree to this, you're a whore."

I didn't say anything for a long time. She didn't apologize, but she changed the subject. She asked me where I got my new flare jeans and if we could go shopping on Saturday; the Gap and Jacob were having sales. I said yes, then told her I had to go. I had a lot to think about.

I kept messing around with him, of course.

"I think we'll be doing this forever," he said. "I think we'll get married—to other people—and still be messing around." He laughed, and even though what he was suggesting was both of us cheating on someone else, what I heard was, us, forever.

I had selective hearing and selective amnesia.

I had denial down to an art form.

OUR LAST TIME BEFORE HE MET SARAH WAS IN A CLASSROOM. WE were pretending to study for our English exam after having written a history one. We were alone. He shut the door. I sat at one of the desks, and he stood behind me. I could feel his breath at the back of my neck. He opened my poetry book to a random page. I skimmed it quickly. It was a poem about a miner's wife. We pretended to scan it for literary devices.

"Look, here's some alliteration," I said.

He put his hand down my shirt. His fingers were in my bra when we thought we heard someone walking by. My heart was beating so fast. Neither of us said a word. When he kissed me then, full of urgency, I felt more connected to him then I ever had to anybody.

After, I was so happy I caught the wrong bus home. I was half an hour from where I lived before I realized I was heading in the wrong direction.

That night, when I described it to Bethany on the phone, my dad overheard me. Actually, what he heard was, "then he felt me over my jeans, and it was amazing." He refused to drive me to Jason's house ever again, or give me the phone when he called. He yelled until the veins in his forehead showed. He gave me a used-car analogy about my body that hurt the most: why in the world anyone would want a crappy, overused model, when they could get a new one for free? He told me I'd be alone forever. I was starting to wonder if that was true.

LAST WEEK BETHANY AND I WERE WATCHING *DAWSON'S CREEK.* We were at our own houses, portable phones resting on her desk and my plastic blow-up couch, as we waited for the show to be over so we could talk again. We watched as Joey expressed how much she loved Dawson. She said how much he meant to her, how she'd wait for him for as long as he needed to realize how much he loved her too. They were meant to be together, she knew it.

"That's how I feel about Jason," I said, fighting back tears.

I heard her take a breath. She was waiting, pausing dramatically so her words would have more effect. "He doesn't love you back, Katie," she said matter-of-factly. She claimed that she was so harsh because she was worried about me. Because she could see things that I couldn't. I knew the truth: she was being cruel because she was a bitch. She didn't give a shit about how I felt. I hung up the phone on her.

I TRY TO AVOID JASON FOR THE REST OF THE DAY, AND I MOSTLY manage. I avoid Bethany after she tells me at lunch that my shirt is too low cut.

"You're sending out the wrong message, Katie," she says.

I go to Speedy's for dinner, and his parents pour me some wine with my dinner. It makes me dizzy. When we're sitting alone in his room after dinner, Speedy tries to make a move. He puts his hand on my thigh. He tries to kiss me. He tells me I need to get over Jason, that he can help. I push him off me. I'm so angry I can't see.

Speedy's dad drives me home. I think he's starting to figure it out, because he asks me three times if I want him to go inside with me. I say no—I insist—because, for one thing, it's embarrassing and, for another, my parents would never do anything in front of anyone, so I'd look like a liar. But more than that, it's a messy situation, and he can't help. No one can.

When I get home my parents are waiting for me in the living room.

In case you've never had a vase smashed in your face, let me describe it. You close your eyes and feel shards of glass on your cheeks and eyelids. You're afraid to open your eyes in case when you do you go blind, so you just stand there with your head ringing.

I feel hot blood run down the side of my face. I have a headache already. I shake myself and open my eyes slowly, backing down the hall. My dad grabs the huge chest of drawers and slams it into me, hitting me below my chest. It kills. I wish I had more natural padding, the way walls have insulation. I wish I had a gun, or a knife, a good way to defend myself. My mom's screaming at me, and my dad rams the chest of drawers into me again. I try to find something to focus on. I think of cartoons, loud music. I fantasize about being a rock star, playing electric guitar to an adoring audience.

When they finally stop I back into a corner of my bedroom, turn the lights off, and close the door. I know they'll be exhausted, too exhausted to follow me into my room, too tired to say or do anything more.

In three months I graduate from high school. When my friends go off to university and start their lives I'm going to start mine too. I'm going to get the fuck out of here. I'm never going to speak to my parents again, never going to need or take anything from them again, ever. It's just going to be me, and I'm going to be fine.

I've always wanted to live in a quieter city, in a place with more artists and fewer business people. I've always wanted to live by the sea. I've always wanted to have real friends. When I finish school, I'm leaving. I'm going to hitchhike if I have to, sleep in the backs of trucks, swim, boat, fly, whatever it takes to get to Victoria. What I want is a life that feels like my own, where I can be myself, and not the things that happened to me.

What I want more than anything is the chance to start over. To face the future without a past. To figure out what I really want, and just, quietly, do it.

MY SO-CALLED DATE

★

I GOT REALLY DRUNK ONCE. I GOT SO DRUNK THAT I THOUGHT I was going to die, and I kind of hoped I would. I was fourteen, downed too much tequila at a house party, and spent all night puking on everything in sight. I even peed in the middle of a public street.

I haven't touched alcohol since.

I never tell this story to anyone because I like to pretend there's some punk-rock reason why I don't drink. I'm way too young to have gotten into Minor Threat, so it's not like I'm straight edge. I definitely could be though: I could rock a couple X's on my hands, preach poetic about the evils of alcohol and promiscuous sex. I tell people I don't drink, but I never tell them why. I try to come off casual, like I'm kidding around, but the truth is, I don't like drinking. I hate the burning taste of alcohol in my throat and stomach, and I hate not being in control. I'm such a wuss. It's like the time I broke my leg in three places riding my bike when I was twelve.

I haven't ridden a bike since.

I'M TWENTY-ONE, AND I'M SITTING WITH A GUY AT THE BLACK Bull at Queen West and Soho. His name is Jack. He's a screenwriter and movie producer.

I'm already annoyed because I can't order anything off the menu. I'm a longtime vegetarian and, besides, I'm health conscious. I think anything deep-fried is deeply disgusting. I live down the street at Queen and John, so his choice of location totally lacks imagination. It's a regular hipster hangout and pub, but because it's Olympics season, it's turned into a sports bar. Everyone is staring, riveted, at the flat screen TVs—yelling, throwing things, getting so caught up in something so ridiculous. I mean, if they were jocks I could understand, but this place is packed with scenesters— guys sporting faux hawks and girls wearing ironic metal-band T-shirts—loudly cheering for the Canadian women's gymnastics team. It's actually kind of funny.

JACK SHOWED UP TO OUR FIRST DATE AT A COFFEE SHOP wearing huge silver-rimmed sunglasses and a black leather jacket. He had the rock-star look down with none of the attitude. He was modest, which is always sexy. I congratulated him on some of his successes and he shrugged, said he didn't think it was a big deal. He was already thinking ahead to his next few projects—pretty ambitious for a guy of twenty-three. I played him some music that I liked and he listened intently—turning the volume up on my iPod headphones, staring ahead without looking at me, concentrating. I wished I were a song so he would give me that kind of attention.

When he got up I noticed how gangly and awkward he was—6' 1" and skinny—but that just added to his charm. It made me believe his bad-boy look was just a veneer, that underneath he was a sweet guy who just wanted to be understood. He held open the door for me on my way in and paid for my tea before we left. It was decided: I liked him. I called him later and invited him over the next week. I guess you could say we got to know each other better.

I REACH OUT ACROSS THE TABLE AND TRY TO HOLD JACK'S HAND. He holds mine for a minute, then drops it and looks away. He didn't call me for more than a week after we slept together. I was really upset because I started to think I'd never hear from him again.

He finally called me this morning.

"Hi Janie," he said, making me instantly melt. I had told him how I feel about being called Jane all the time. It always sounds like everyone's mad at me. Like I'm waiting for the rest of the sentence: "Jane Marie Campbell, clean up your room!" I was so happy he'd been listening. He asked if he could take me out tonight, if we could go for drinks.

I'm pretty sure I also told him I don't drink. But here I am. I wanted to show him that I was laid back and cool, that I could hang out after we'd had sex, like it was no big deal. I wanted to show him that I didn't need a commitment right away, even though I was secretly hoping for one.

A waitress wearing a tiny black skirt and a really low-cut shirt comes by to take our order. She's got short, red, streaked hair and a lip ring. I feel like I'm in an alternative Hooters. I don't know why he wanted to meet here, of all places. I told him I wanted to spend more time with him, so I figure maybe we'll go somewhere else after. I kind of hope he'll come over again. I figure he'll at least want to fool around. I have no objections.

WHEN HE CAME TO MY APARTMENT THAT FIRST NIGHT I SAID I wanted to show him my paintings. I have my work plastered and taped in sketched and finished form all over my walls. I don't know how to describe them; they're bright and abstract with a lot of geometric shapes. I care about colour more than anything else and there's a lot of emotional subtext. He asked me who my influences were and I told him Matisse and Picasso, plus a contemporary artist named Cecily Brown.

I wanted him to like my work. I wanted him to value it on a technical level—but more than that I wanted it to move him. I wanted him to look at my art and magically see into the depths of my soul. I wanted him to see the anguish, the hurt, the vulnerability, and I wanted him to tell me it was okay. I wanted him to tell me that I was okay.

I was surprised when he did. He stared at the paintings, seemingly fascinated, and told me they were amazing. I don't know if I believed him, but it was nice that he could see what I needed to hear and he was willing to give it to me. I took it as a sign that he cared about how I felt. He really piled it on, giving me compliment after compliment. I found it hard to resist—I hadn't painted in a while and I needed the encouragement.

I LOOK AT HIM NOW, WAITING FOR HIM TO SAY SOMETHING NICE. He orders a beer and I sigh. I order a glass of water. He's so bad at making conversation. He tells me he likes my earrings—they're long and dangling, with little blue beads and silver hearts. I got them for five bucks in Kensington Market. It's such a strange thing for him to notice.

That's exactly how he was when he came over. He was so obvious, so klutzy in his approach that I felt I could trust him. He didn't seem like a player, like he had the charm or skill to get with a lot of women. So that night I just came right out and said it. I told him I liked him.

He looked a little embarrassed, but happy. "I really like you, too," he said, "and I really want to," pulling me onto his lap, "but I have a girlfriend," he added, reaching for my hand.

I didn't know what to say. I asked him how long they'd been together and he told me only a couple of months. Our faces were so close and my other hand was resting on his leg. He kissed me, and I didn't try to stop him.

Now I slide my foot under the table and start kicking his feet. I take off one of my sandals and slide my left ankle up his calf. He smiles and doesn't say anything. I think of leaning over and asking him if he wants to meet me in the bathroom.

It moved so fast last time. One minute we were making out, the next we stumbled from the couch to my bed. I had to peel myself off the black leather and let him drag me, hanging onto his black-and-white baseball T-shirt. He moved his tongue in such a weird way. I felt it on the roof of my mouth and on my teeth. I wasn't having a great time, but I wasn't scared either. I slid under the covers to take my clothes off. I didn't want him to see me naked. He inched closer and closer beside me. I felt the skin of his thighs brush up against mine.

I made him stop because I realized something. Of course I didn't have any condoms. He said he'd go out and get some while he ran some errands. He said he had to do that stuff anyway, plus he didn't want our first time to be rushed. *Wow, our first time*, I thought. *That's so sweet.* I wanted to start having sex again. I wanted to rejoin the human race.

I MADE MY EX-BOYFRIEND WAIT A LONG TIME TO HAVE SEX. When I was finally ready, he decorated his apartment on Isabella Street with tons of candles, and there were roses and white wine when I walked in the door.

"I want it to be perfect for you," he said, like he was talking to someone else.

We lay down on his mattress and made out. I remember

how his hair felt to the touch; my hands were shaking when they brushed his cheeks. I'd psyched myself up, done all the things you're supposed to do: I'd gone to the free clinic and gotten birth control pills, I'd bought condoms, I'd thought about what it would be like . . . But I was so scared. I kept stopping and getting up, walking around his tiny bachelor apartment. I told him I loved him, that I hoped he'd understand. He looked me in the eye, forcefully, and told me he loved me, like he was trying to convince me of something. I got back in bed, but it just didn't feel right.

"So when do we get to make love?" he asked impatiently

"I-I don't know," I stammered, trying to move onto my side. I didn't want to face him. I tried to get up and found that I couldn't, he'd locked his legs onto mine and I couldn't move. He was on top of me, looking down at me with a terrible look in his eyes, like he was about to sink his teeth into me.

"Spread your legs," he said in a low tone.

I didn't want to. I know I said no.

"It'll be over fast," he said, unzipping his jeans and tearing my underwear. I felt a searing pain almost immediately. It made me wish I'd paid attention in biology class. I never expected sex to hurt so much. I couldn't understand why people did it. So much risk—pregnancy and STDs, a boyfriend who plunges into you without a condom, without protection, without your permission.

It felt like it lasted at least fifteen minutes, but he later told me it was five. When he was done I crawled into his bathroom, lay down on the beige ceramic tiles, and didn't move for what felt like hours. I locked the door behind me and cried, trying to figure out how I could leave without him seeing me. I crawled out the window onto his balcony. It was January, and I was standing there in just my T-shirt, no pants or underwear. My tears were starting to freeze on my cheeks.

I yelled out into the street until the woman in the apartment next door heard me. She told me to climb over onto her balcony and come inside. She wrapped a wool blanket around me, and I stood in her living room shivering, teeth chattering. I had no idea what she was saying.

She loaned me a sweater and a pair of black spandex leggings I assume she didn't expect to get back. She gave me money for a taxi, and I sat staring out of the frost-coated car window, breathing on it, tracing circles with my fingers.

JACK CAME BACK TO MY APARTMENT TWO HOURS LATER WITH condoms. I can't say it was a great experience. It hurt a lot, more than I thought it would. I felt skin tearing, and I was surprised there was anything left to tear. I lay there waiting for it to be over, wondering why I wasn't enjoying it more. I felt like such a freak. Like I was the only person in the world who doesn't really love sex. I wondered if I would ever enjoy it. I tried to talk to him about it after—about how I was feeling. I tried to tell him what was on my mind. I could tell he thought it was too much, too soon, but he tried to be polite.

He fell asleep, and I spent five hours staring at the ceiling in the dark. I didn't want to snore. I didn't want to take up too much room in the bed. The next morning he left early. I was half asleep as I walked him to the door. He said he'd call me on the weekend and we'd make plans. I told him Saturday was good. I spent the whole day waiting for the phone to ring.

I'M ANNOYED IT TOOK HIM SO LONG TO CALL ME, BUT I'M STILL glad to be here. I'm suddenly self-conscious about the clothes I'm wearing: a tube top and a short skirt that hits just above my knees. You can see my calves and some of my thighs when I sit. You can also see my shoulders and some of my cleavage. He hasn't appeared to notice, though. There are guys who look at you like they're taking you in, like they're observing you—like they really care. This guy keeps looking around me and beside me, but not directly at me. It's making me feel nervous and guilty—as if I'm doing something wrong by wanting to be with him.

He's wearing ripped jeans. They're not cool new jeans with a couple of small, casually ripped holes. They're jeans that look like they're ten years old with missing kneecaps and holes in the ass. He's sporting a T-shirt that says *Come to the Bahamas*. It's white with little grey dolphins on it. Maybe he got dressed in the dark.

"Jane," I hear him say sharply, "aren't you going to order anything?"

I shake my head. He's calling me Jane now. It sounds so cold, dashed off without even an afterthought. I really hate my name. Jane and Finch, Jane Doe, Jane Seymour. Actually, I take that back; Jane Lane was the coolest character on *Daria*. I still hate *Dr. Quinn, Medicine Woman*, though.

My so-called date orders a BLT and I want to vomit. White bread, mayonnaise, bacon. Gross. Why not just inject it into your veins? I make a face and our alterna-whore waitress sees it and smiles. She gets it. She probably sees it enough in here: guys that are trying to use girls, girls that are going along for the ride.

He orders his second beer. "I'm Scottish," he says and leaves it at that. *Uh, okay.*

I wish I were here with someone who really understood me. I wish I were here with someone I could open up to. I want to tell him what it was like to be violated by someone I trusted. I want to tell him that there was so much more to it than rape.

WHEN I GOT BACK TO MY PARENTS' HOUSE THAT NIGHT I WENT to the bathroom and found myself bleeding. I had no idea if I had my period, if I was going to get my period, if I could be pregnant. I had to sneak off to a Planned Parenthood the next day to take a morning-after pill.

It never occurred to me that I needed to get tested for STDs. Apparently, you have to wait at least three months after having sex for an HIV test. I found myself sitting in an AIDS clinic downtown with my best friend, who sat there squeezing my arm, convincing me that I wasn't going to die.

"Even if you do have it," he joked, "you'll have at least five years."

I didn't know if I wanted to laugh or kill him. Thank God I didn't have anything. I definitely had reason to worry. My ex-boyfriend had just informed me that he'd been with prostitutes—a couple a year since '96. He'd originally told me that he'd had five partners. "Oh, I don't count the whores," he said casually.

THE WAITRESS COMES BACK AND REFILLS MY WATER. I REALIZE that Jack's been talking this whole time and I haven't even been listening. I have no idea what he's talking about. You'd think he'd notice.

I ask him why he got into movies. He seems to love art, but he does a lot of blockbusters. The waitress brings his food and he starts wolfing it down, ketchup dripping through his fingers, French fries flying.

"It's the money," he says, mouth full.

It turns out he wants a big house just like his dad's.

"Sorry, I'm just really hungry," he continues, sending spit flying. I think of asking him if he wants a shovel. Hey, I could use a shovel. I could beat him over the head with it and bury him in my backyard. No one would know.

He doesn't realize what a big deal it is that I'm here right now. I never thought I'd recover this much. I never thought

I'd find myself wearing clothes like this, at a normal weight, on a date with a guy I hardly know. It's been six months since it happened and sometimes I still freak out when I get attention from guys. I've hyperventilated walking down the street, thinking guys were checking me out.

I went through a phase of wanting to cover up my body— every extra curve or ounce of flesh made me feel more vulnerable. I believed that having a womanly body made me attractive and vulnerable to predators, and in order to be safe, the less of it I had the better. I didn't want to be a woman; I didn't want to have a body. I stopped eating until I landed myself in hospital two months ago. I spent two weeks lying in bed staring at white walls and white ceilings. I wouldn't eat so they had to strap an IV into my arm.

I turned the corner when an art therapist named Wendy came to see me.

"I heard you used to paint a lot," she said.

"Yeah, used to," I answered. I hadn't done anything since I'd gotten sick.

She left a sketch pad and pencil next to my bed. A few days later I drew something. It was a girl with a rail thin body—just a few lines with a face on top. Beside her were the words *I want to be free*. I hadn't even realized that I wanted to come back. I didn't know I had any fight left. Forget the bullshit they tell you about how once you're anorexic you never get over it. I weigh 125 pounds now.

I WAS REALLY HAPPY WHEN JACK WANTED TO SLEEP WITH ME. I just wish he wanted me right now. He's finished eating, and I want to leave this place. I want him to come over to my apartment and make me feel desirable and wanted again. I want to have sex again, and I want it to hurt less this time. I want to keep doing it until it doesn't hurt at all and I like it and I'm normal. I want him to be nice to me, hold my hand and compliment me until I'm over this thing that was so unfair, this thing that I know I didn't deserve. I want to relax and not suspect every guy I meet. I want to be who I was before.

"Do you want to come over now?" I ask him as sweetly as possible.

"I can't," he tells me quickly. "Anyway, I have to be out of here in a hour."

I can't believe him. "Why, where are you going?" I ask kind of harshly.

"I have to meet my girlfriend," he says, not looking at me. So he's chosen her.

I wonder if I did anything wrong. If I had too many problems, if I was too intense.

"You're a really intimate person," he says, trying to meet my gaze. He says it gently, but the implication is clear. He thinks it's a bad thing.

I bite my lip to keep from crying. "She's probably waiting for you," I say, staring at the table. "You should go now."

I hear the sound of metal grazing wood as he pulls his

chair out. He gets up to walk out, quickly pays the tab. I don't do anything to stop him.

"I don't ever want to speak to you again," I whisper, not sure if he can hear me.

I look up and see the small of his back as he heads through the swinging doors. I try to smile and feel relieved.

LUCKY

★

WHEN I WAS A KID, LIKE TEN OR ELEVEN OR SOMETHING, I WON a contest in a pizzeria for a drawing I did of the characters from *The Simpsons*. It was at this cheesy Italian restaurant in a mall that had melting red wax candles at every table and baskets of bread sticks on red and white checked table cloths. They were trying to pull in families with kids, so every month they had a new contest. I had to draw my favourite TV show. I won a life-sized version of Maggie Simpson, and my family kept telling me how lucky I was.

When I was in grade six I cheated on a surprise test my social studies teacher gave us. I got an A, but the boy sitting next to me, who was skinny with delicate hands and thick glasses took the blame when the teacher asked us why our answers were exactly the same. It was my first time cheating, so I didn't know you were supposed to paraphrase. I knew I was lucky. When he asked me out I told him my parents wouldn't let me date yet, and I tried to be extra nice to him in class. You never know when you'll need someone again.

Last year, when I was sixteen, I bought a couple of

scratch- and-win cards, and one time I won $5,000. I spent it so fast it's not even funny. The women at the clothing store couldn't believe how much I was buying. They were falling all over themselves to help me, and it was a great feeling. I felt powerful, like a rich Hollywood star, like I should've been on the cover of *Teen People*, or *Teen Vogue*, showing off my closets while they took glamorous pictures of me.

I felt really lucky.

I WAS FIFTEEN WHEN I MET HIM. ACTUALLY, TECHNICALLY, I WAS sixteen when we met, but fifteen when we first started talking. We met online. I said on my page that I was single, and I guess he liked the photo of me. My hair was in a ponytail, and I was wearing my brother's baseball hat backwards. I thought it looked cool, but I was being kind of ironic. I was making a face, sticking my tongue out, and my eyes looked kind of small because I was laughing, even though I was trying to look cool. He told me he liked it right away.

There was another one of me blowing a huge bubble of grape Bubblicious, and it exploding all over my face. The second time we talked he told me it was his favourite. I looked like I was having a good time, he said, going wild and looking scared and kind of vulnerable at the same time. That's when I decided I kind of liked him too. He seemed smart, like a good observer. Plus, he was hot, and the guys at my school were really boring. I didn't want to date any of them. I turned two down, and then the rest stopped asking, which was okay, because I wasn't interested anyway. What-ever. Internet dating was the thing, everyone knew, and my town had three other high schools anyway.

He told me his real name right away. I mean, everyone called him Spence, or Spenny, but that made him cringe and I could understand why. He wanted me to call him Spencer. He called me a week later, and we talked for, like, four hours, non-stop. It was awesome. We figured out that we both love *South Park* and *The Simpsons*, and the same music and ev-erything. He went to the high school really near to where I lived. I wanted to go there too, but my parents said it was a shitty school. The thing is, it was in our neighborhood, which is really safe, so it didn't make sense.

He came over, and we played Game Cube and hung out in the backyard and he pushed me on the swing, which was super romantic and cute. That night my family had a bar-beque, and they invited him to stay. He'd only kissed me once, before anyone else had gotten home, but later he groped me on the staircase when no one else was watching. It was awesome. He put one hand on the railing, and moved his other arm like he was going to reach over me, but then he put his hand down my shirt instead.

Spencer was the first person to ever agree with me that my parents were fucking nuts. My parents were Christians. They made me go to church ever single Sunday of my life, wear stupid white dresses, sit with my legs crossed, all that crap. I went to Bible camp, learned all the hymns by heart, always had to say grace before meals, the whole mother-fucking nine yards.

I wasn't allowed to date or fool around with guys, and I promised my parents more than once that I would wait till I was married to fuck someone. It would be all about the wedding night, procreation, God's gift, etc. My older brother wasn't even allowed to jack off. Apparently, wasting sperm is a sin. What a goddamn stupid idea, if you ask me. It's all so freaking unnatural. But I also suck at self-control. I'm really glad I'm naturally thin, 'cause I could never diet. And I could never bring myself to go to the gym.

I'm lucky I can get away without it.

FOR A WHILE MY PARENTS LIKED SPENCER. HE EVEN CAME WITH us to church once, and lied about how the minister's sermon had moved him, while I tried to sleep through it with my eyes wide open. He was polite, and he knew how to work adults. He was two years older than me, so he had more experience with that. He was eighteen, and almost done high school. He knew how to BS them about what he planned to do with his life, how he planned to become rich and successful and wonderful and charitable, and all that.

I still had to lie to my parents though, telling them I was sleeping at a friend's, 'cause they couldn't know I was going to his house at night, or sleeping over. His mom was a single mom and didn't give a shit. I think she liked me, actually. She seemed like she did. We smoked cigarettes together and she made me my first Irish coffee one morning. She was awesome, now that I think about it.

EVERYTHING TURNED TO SHIT THE FIRST TIME MY PARENTS caught me lying. They called my friend Yvette, wanting to know where I was, and she was too scared to lie for me and nearly shat her pants or something and told them. Just like that, she sold me out. Some friend—I've known her since, like, kindergarten. Apparently, she told my parents that Spencer was a bad influence on me, and didn't they know that he went to Grove Heights, which was full of gangs and juvenile delinquents? It turns out they didn't.

From then on my parents forbade me to see him, which was fine, I just lied to them. Then they overheard me in the bathroom one night talking to him on my cellphone.

My mom slapped me across the face. My dad left high-lighted articles about teenage crime waves and gangs on the desk where I did my homework. They started questioning me before I did anything. I had to tell them before I went anywhere, including to the bathroom during dinner. My life started feeling like a prison.

I didn't feel so lucky anymore.

It was around that time that Spencer first told me he loved me. I used to ditch third and fourth period and hang out with him until after lunch. Sometimes I ditched the whole day, but I was so good at forging notes that no one ever caught me.

"Why are your parents so stupid?" he asked me one day, after they'd spent two hours yelling at me about my grades on a history final. "When the fuck would you ever need this shit?" he said about the dumb American history I'd failed to memorize. He was so supportive and so nice.

"Let's run away together," he said, and at first I laughed, but then he told me he was serious. That summer we were going to Canada. We were going to cross the border in British Columbia and live out in the forest, in nature. We had it all planned. It was going to be perfect. I wouldn't need to finish high school. We'd have each other. We'd make love and be in love.

That night when my parents asked me where I was going, and I told them I was going to Spencer's, all hell broke loose. You'd think I just told them I joined a cult. They went fucking nuts. My dad threw the book he was reading at me, and it hit me in the head. I got a bump almost instantly. That's the thing: people thought my dad was this great soft, gentle respectable guy, but he was an asshole. No one had any idea.

When I got to Spencer's I was so angry and upset. He gave me some beer, and we did a little acid, but that was all. When I told him the story, he got so mad. We drove over to my parents so he could confront them.

He yelled at my dad, and then he shot him in the head. He got him right in the bullseye, in the temple, I think. He dropped right away. My mom stood there, shaking and frozen, and then she screamed. Her eyes rolled back in her head like ping pong balls. It was scary, like she was looking at nothing. Spencer shot her in the chest.

Gunshots sound like fireworks, a little. You get this little surge of adrenaline, like the shot before a race starts. You feel like you can run and run, you want to jump up and down, but just as you do, something stops you from looking like an ass. I just stood there and stared for a long time. I couldn't believe they were dead.

I guess I was free. I felt some kind of relief, euphoria, and then fear. Hard, cold, fucking fear. Getting caught. What the hell would our story be?

I felt vomit at the back of my throat. I think Spencer caught me right before I fainted. His fingerprints were all over the place. He confessed to the police, while I cried and held onto him, and begged them to take me with him.

Because I was under eighteen, I was protected by the Young Offenders Act. The general public doesn't know my name, and I won't have a criminal record. I still sometimes think that I love Spencer, sometimes I think I love him more than ever.

The thing is, he's in jail now, awaiting trial. He stirred up all these feelings in me, all this confusion, and sometimes I really don't know what I feel. That's all I wanted, I guess, to feel special and unique. Apparently that's normal. Apparently lots of girls do. In a way, I blame my parents.

They never understood how really lucky I am.

THE PREGNANT MAN

★

BEING PREGNANT IS NOTHING LIKE I THOUGHT IT WOULD BE. I expected it to be moving, life-affirming. I knew that my hormones would go up and down, that it would be an emotional time. I read all those books, the classics: *What to Expect When You're Expecting*, *The Girlfriend's Guide to Pregnancy*, all that stuff. I'd read it all, from the mainstream stuff to the queer-friendly stuff. I knew all about morning sickness, loss of appetite, and strange cravings; strange looks and unwanted attention. I knew I'd get fat, that my body would change, that my ankles and wrists would swell. I knew I'd sometimes look in the mirror and not recognize myself. I knew it all, but still, it was harder than I thought it would be.

I WAS A TOMBOYISH KID WHO PLAYED SPORTS AND HATED dresses, but lots of girls are like that; it doesn't mean anything. I liked guys, but as buddies, confidants, players on a team. I guess I was about fourteen or so when I first realized. It wasn't overnight. Things dawned on me slowly, tiny realizations that finally led to a conclusion that was so simple, it was painful. I was gay. *Whatever*, I thought. I was kind of glad to have it figured out. No denial, dating guys, or self-delusion.

That was that.

I started fantasizing about girls when I was fifteen. I bought dirty girlie magazines and hid them under my bed. I had sticky fingertips from thinking about hot brunettes. When I saw a girl at school I found attractive—because she was smart, because she was hot, because she was kind—my legs would shake. After gym class, girls would gossip, walking around in their panties and bras, chatting to me, treating me like one of them, and I was racked with guilt. If only they knew what I was thinking. If only they knew I was wishing I had a camera with me just then. If only they knew that I was taking them in, angle by soft angle, part by part. If only they knew I'd be thinking about them all night.

When I eyed the guys at my school, I couldn't even fake it. I felt nothing, nothing in my heart, in my head, below my waist. I didn't find teenage boys disgusting or gross, because I was one of them. I listened to them talk about wanting to bang girls with envy. I wanted to do that too: I wanted to do it and then boast and swagger like they did. I didn't want to be a bad person, I didn't want to lead anyone on, or use anyone, but I did want gratification in the same way. I wanted to get laid, and I wanted that to be okay.

WHEN I WAS SIXTEEN MY PARENTS MOVED AND I GOT transferred to another school. The summer before, I discovered punk rock. I listened non-stop to the Clash and the Ramones and Black Flag. My favourite Clash song was "Lost in the Supermarket." It made me feel like less of an outsider. I went to a punk club downtown and saw lots of chicks that looked the way I wanted to: dyed, short haircuts, torn clothes, androgynous. There were hot girls in short red kilts and tiny tube tops, and I knew it was my scene.

Finding other people like me made it easier. Just knowing they existed. I chopped my hair off with a razor I found in my parent's bathroom. I got a friend, this girl Cleo, to help me dye it, first with Tie Dye, then with Kool-Aid, then finally with Manic Panic, which was expensive and had to keep being redone.

I made out with Cleo two weeks after that and dated her on and off for a year. She was a high school dropout, but one of the smartest people I'd ever met. We'd skip class and walk around downtown and smoke weed and get into bars and sit there in the middle of the day, nursing beers, trying to look adult. She'd always tell me how guy-like I was, how I swaggered like a guy, how I had a gut and no hips like a guy. She liked my broad shoulders. She teased me, told me I'd be the football star in my school—if I'd just been born with a dick. She always called me her quarterback.

Whenever she talked like that I'd laugh, but it hurt, and I'd pretend it didn't. I was angry all the time—like a teenage guy, I guess. I body-slammed myself into walls, punched my locker when I was having a bad day. It just seemed so unfair to me, like why the hell was I made a woman when I was clearly a man? I couldn't figure it out. The thing is, even though I had a girlfriend and parents who pretended not to notice or didn't actually know or care what I was doing, I wasn't an idiot. I knew the stigma attached to being gay. I knew how I'd be treated by teachers, the principal, the stupid close-minded community I lived in when I actually came out with it. And yet I did it. I was what I was. There was nothing I could do. I was attracted to and wanted to be with women. But I felt like and wanted to be a man.

WHEN I WAS IN COLLEGE I MET A WOMAN. HER NAME WAS Barbara, and she was three years older than me. She was delicate and feminine and beautiful. I wrote her love letters.

When we made love, I was always scared she'd break. I tried to control the urge to hold her like she was a piece of glass. Whenever she left my room she left a trail of lingering perfume, Gaultier, or sometimes Elizabeth Arden.

She was an English literature major, a well-read, intelligent, classy woman. I never understood what she was doing with me. When she left me after a year and a half, she told me what I'd always known, what I always knew. That I was a college experiment to her. She wanted to be with a man, she said, who was both as sensitive and as masculine as I was. I hope she found him.

I didn't date for a long time after that, aside from the occasional one-night stand at a pub night or a late-night study session. I have never, to this day, been with a guy. I've never wanted to. I've always known I wouldn't be missing anything.

I MET AIMEE A FEW YEARS LATER, WHEN I WAS TWENTY-SEVEN and she was twenty-five. I met her at work, through one of my colleagues. It was pretty mundane and unromantic actually, a classic set-up story. She had shoulder-length brown hair and blue eyes. She was beautiful and smart and funny. We moved in together after three months.

She supported me when I started taking hormone treatments. When I grew hair on my chest, she played with it, stroked it, said she loved it. When my breasts disappeared, when I grew a mustache, then a beard, and went up two clothing sizes, she just said there was more of me to love, and I could tell she meant it. I always knew she was it for me, I just knew it.

When I changed my name from Antonia to Anthony, which basically meant that I was still Toni, just spelled with a Y now, she just laughed. I kept my vagina in fairness to her, though. She was grateful. But I felt like a man, and I still do.

We got married after a year, and I'd never been happier. We bought a dog, and then our condo. My life felt perfect.

Then two years ago, she told me that she wanted to have a kid. We talked about donors, then ended up at a clinic, choosing from lists of men. We spent a fortune, giving it shot after shot at different clinics, trying different kinds of fertility treatments, until an expert told us it was no use. Aimee couldn't have a baby.

We racked our brains. The doctor suggested adoption, and we looked into seriously. Then Aimee explained to him about me, that I was still technically a woman, that it might be possible for me to conceive.

We were elated and terrified. We didn't sleep for weeks. We were up all night, talking or arguing or pacing. We took turns sleeping on the couch, crying to our friends, thinking about breaking up or going straight. I thought about getting a full-blown sex change and making all of this impossible. We spent a lot of money. Thousands, in retrospect. Tens of thousands, even. I miscarried three times, went on and off my hormones . . .

FINALLY, I'M PREGNANT AND HEALTHY. SOMETIMES I FEEL SO grateful I want to cry, and other times I just feel like an ass. I have a hairy chest and back pain and stomach aches and nausea and cravings for sour food. On the street I'm torn between wearing extra large clothes to cover up; acting like a couch potato, chip-eating oaf who just got fat; and being proud of the freak show I've become. Sometimes I'm so embarrassed I cry. Other times I feel overwhelmingly proud and compassionate toward all women who go through this. It's a miracle for Aimee and me, but it's a regular rite of passage for women all over the world. It's nothing, just carrying a living being. Giving birth, giving life. Sometimes I can't stand the waves of emotions I feel. It's too much sometimes. There are days when I can't leave the house.

When we give birth to our daughter, we want to name her Mirari. It means miracle in Portuguese, which is Aimee's background. She will be our miracle, and we will be her family, no matter what anyone thinks. After she's born, I'll get that sex change. I'll finally be a man. And when she's old enough to know, I'll tell her. I'll tell her that her dad, her old man, was the world's first pregnant man. I hope she won't think it's a punch line. I hope she'll be able to love me and accept me no matter what. I already know how much I love her.

JUST FRIENDS

★

IT WAS OVER. SHE HAD RUN AWAY, GONE ACROSS THE WORLD
to Australia to be in a band. It was a huge opportunity,
blah blah blah. They had always known it was coming, he
supposed; it was one of those unspoken things they both
knew was there. He had secretly hoped that since she never
brought it up, she would change her mind. She had avoided
it for only one reason: she didn't want to disappoint him and
break his heart, but she knew she would.

It wasn't that she didn't love him; for the better part of
three years she was more than positive that she did. There
were times when she was sure she loved him so much that
it physically hurt her. On those nights, when she lay in her
single bed waiting for him, wondering if he was with someone else, wondering what would happen to them, wondering if he really loved her, she was convinced her heart would
burst. He'd put her through a lot in the beginning, but she'd
stayed with him.

He knew he'd made her wait a long time. He remem-
bered the first time she told him she loved him. They were

drunk. She had a dark red ring of wine around her mouth. She touched his hair around his ear. She made eye contact then stared out the window. He thought she was just saying it; they'd only known each other a few months. Afterward, he wondered if she knew him well enough to mean it. He suspected that she didn't. Maybe she wanted it to be true. Maybe, on some level, he did too.

She knew he wasn't ready, but that one day he would be—so she waited. She cried a lot. She got drunk with her friends and made out with random boys in clubs. Her friends took pictures and bragged to him on her behalf. She was trying to hurt him, but he never showed her how he felt. He'd shrug his shoulders. He'd tell her they weren't committed to each other, that she was free. She didn't feel free. She felt anchored down, bound to her feelings against her will. She tried to take space for herself. She took holidays with friends. She didn't talk to him for weeks. She went on dates with guys who had real jobs, guys who took her to dinner and bought her presents. Her mom even met and liked a couple of them. She thought it would be so much easier to have feelings for one of those generic guys, and she tried to, but she couldn't make herself.

He spent a lot of time alone. He read a whole collection of plays. He drew. Sometimes he got drunk with the guys, and other times he hung out with his female friends. Sometimes he hung out with them one on one, other times in groups of three or four or five. He called them *honey* and *darling*. It was easier because they didn't mean anything to him. When he spoke to her, he called her by her name. Petra. His lips popped over the P. She liked the way he said it. He made it sound beautiful, exotic even.

She was jealous. She spent hours dissecting the conversations she overhead him having on his cellphone. It ate her alive, made her feel less special, not just to him, but as a person. It made her question who she was, what the point of her life was. It made her hate those girls, and hate herself for feeling that way. She wondered if he'd slept with or made out with any of them. She asked herself if it mattered. Were any of those girls in love with him too, had they told him and he pretended he hadn't heard them either. Would they continue to pursue him, sit waiting, even while they pretended they weren't. They were all intelligent, like her. She knew because she knew them all.

It took him a while, but he woke up. She was finally dating one guy more seriously than she had any of the others, and it hit him. If he didn't get over his fears, his bullshit, his past, he would lose her. *I mean, enough with the self-pity*, he told himself. *Get ahold of yourself, man. Go get the girl.* So he did. It took some work, some winning over. They were deliriously happy for a while. They told everyone how much they loved each other. He felt the need to shout it out, call her his girlfriend, his love. It was like that, then. He wanted to make up for lost time. He had to make it up to her. They both felt it, even though she never said it, never asked him to. But it was there. He had been selfish once, so she re-served the right to walk away anytime.

She hoped he would come with her. Deep down she knew he couldn't. She pretended it hurt less than it did. The truth is, it was the only thing she could do. She was seeing the world, living her dream. She was experiencing all the things she'd read about, visualized, all the things she'd always wanted to do. It was just the beginning, she knew. Just the start of the life she wanted. The thing is, she'd always imag-ined how her life would be with him. She thought they'd get married, have a nice house by the beach, raise kids who were artsy like them, but more practical. He used to picture it with her too, they talked about it all the time. It embar-rassed him, so he didn't admit it, but he liked that picture a whole lot. Loved it, even. Maybe more than she did. Maybe he needed it more.

THEY TALK NOW AND THEN. HE STILL PINES, OCCASIONALLY IN public, and sometimes she tells people, mentions it here and there, but she tries not to. It was her decision. It felt like what she had to do. They still send each other text messages sometimes. They talk on Facebook and MySpace. When people ask, they say there are no hard feelings, then quick-ly change the subject. They always tell people they're still friends. It's easier that way.

ACKNOWLEDGEMENTS

Halli Villegas—for being such an amazing publisher. Thank you for getting what I was trying to do, for believing in it, and taking a chance on me.

Shirarose Wilensky—for being the best editor ever. Thanks for your incredible sensitivity to detail, your vision, and your hard work. Thank you for understanding everything, for asking all the right questions, and for your friendship.

Karen Correia da Silva—for your amazing design work on the cover, and the website. Thank you for sharing your talents, and for adding so much.

And thanks to all the Tightrope interns for all your help

Thanks to: Myna Wallin; Heather Wood, Ed, Joanna, John, and everyone who was part of the Moosemeat Writer's Group; Vanya du Toit for the amazing cover image—I couldn't have imagined anything better (check her out at www.vanyadutoit.blogspot.com); Nino Ricci; Ayelet Waldman; Toast Coetzer; Michelle McGrane; Julia Tausch; Melinda Ferguson; Aryan Kaganof—for so much kindness, encouragement, and inspiration, and thank you for being my friend, above everything; Rosemary Lombard, Cecilia Ferreira, Stella, and the whole Kagablog community for all your help—it means so much to me, you have no idea; John Davies and everyone at Pighog Press in the UK for being so awesome; Colleen Higgs at Modjaji Books in South Africa; Nicole Aube; Sam Hiyate; Damian Rogers for inviting me to read "My So-Called Date" for Pontiac Quarterly (my first reading ever); Richard Scrimger for all your mentoring and help with "Paradox"; everyone at Come on Killer, BWW, and Ons Klyntji; Jannike Bergh at Acoustic Image; Stefan de Witt for the title "Heroin Heights"; Adrian Davies for all the great ideas and stories; Bev Daurio for all your early help and advice; and everyone at Ve'havta and Na-Me-Res, especially Jen.

Many thanks to my family and friends.

Everyone who ever shared their stories and secrets with me—thank you the most.

The title of this book came from a song of the same name by Detroit musician Brendan Benson. Check him out at www.brendanbenson.com.

"My So-Called Date" was first featured at Pontiac Quarterly in the fall of 2006.

"Paradox" first appeared in the South African magazine *Ons Klyntji* in December 2006.

"Don't Talk Junk" first appeared in *Bloody Well Written* in March 2007, and in the Toronto zine *Come On Killer* in the summer of 2007.

"Smacked," "Just Friends," "The Pregnant Man," and "A Tiny Thud" first appeared on the kagablog, www.kaganof.com/kagablog.

The other stories are yours for the very first time. Enjoy.

ABOUT THE AUTHOR

Danila Botha was born in Johannesburg, South Africa. She volunteered with Na-me-res, an organization benefiting the homeless, which inspired many of the stories in *Got No Secrets*. Her writing has appeared in *24 Hours*, *Yoink! Magazine*, and *NOW*. She lives in Halifax.

SUPPORT the UPSTARTS

www.TightropeBooks.com